MISS MOUSE

Mira Stables

FAWCETT COVENTRY • NEW YORK

MISS MOUSE

This book contains the complete text of the original hardcover edition.

Published by Fawcett Coventry Books, a unit of CBS Publications, the Consumer Publishing Division of CBS Inc., by arrangement with Robert Hale Limited

ISBN: 0-449-50178-7

Printed in the United States of America

First Fawcett Coventry printing: April 1981

10 9 8 7 6 5 4 3 2 1

One

His lordship pushed aside the papers with
which he had busied himself while he awaited
Miss Ashley's arrival and rose politely to
greet her, shaking the neatly gloved hand
that she extended to him and accepting her
assurances that her journey had been perfectly comfortable and her refusal of the offer
of refreshment. He dismissed Bosworth, bid-
ding him inform Mrs Palmer of the young
lady's arrival and ask her to appoint one of
the maids to wait upon her in a quarter of an
hour.

"Tell her to send the girl to the library,"
he added. "I daresay Miss Ashley will be glad
of a guide until she becomes accustomed." He

bestowed a disarming smile upon his guest, a smile that successfully concealed the dismay that her appearance had caused him. What maggot had got into his sister's brain to cause her to engage such an odd-looking female?

The children would never take to her. It would be unkind to say that she was actually repulsive, and of course she could not help her appearance. In fact he would concede that, set in a different countenance, her eyes were magnificent. But the sickly pallor of a greasy looking skin, a disfiguring mole at one side of her nose, and an awkwardness in the poor creature's walk and carriage caused by some inequality of the shoulders could not be said to make up an attractive appearance. As matters stood at the moment he had problems enough in keeping a tutor for nephew Benedict. He wondered briefly what had possessed him, in addition, to undertake the charge of his sister's family for a whole summer. His eldest niece, Beatrice, at sixteen, might be expected to behave in reasonably adult fashion. She might even be willing to accept Miss Ashley as a suitable duenna. But he would be willing to stake a handsome sum that Bridget and Adam, the younger children, would have none of her. They would follow Benedict's pattern as they always did. And a boy who was so adept at disposing of tutors would have small difficulty in dealing with this poor little scrap of a governess.

It was really cruel to expose her to such an assault. But what else could he do? Elizabeth had already engaged her. Something to do with her being the sister of an old school friend. He could not dismiss her out of hand. He could only try to strengthen her authority as far as possible. He hoped that at least she had some force of personality to redeem her physical disadvantages.

Once again he was doomed to disappointment. Miss Ashley's voice was flat and unemphatic, and the few platitudes that she uttered were totally devoid of originality. Perhaps she was shy. In an attempt to put her at ease he spoke of his sister, asking if she was well advanced in her preparations for the journey to Copenhagen, and if she was still in raptures at the thought of a 'second honeymoon'.

"I have not had the pleasure of seeing Lady Elizabeth since she attended *my* sister's wedding—and that was three years ago," replied Miss Ashley sedately. "I owe my engagement as governess to my sister's good offices. You are probably aware of the close friendship between them. Bridget knew that I was seeking a new situation and chanced to mention it to Lady Elizabeth who was so good as to say that my close relationship to her friend was sufficient recommendation for the post. It was fortunate, too, that I was able to assume my duties at short notice, since Lady Elizabeth was anxious to travel with her husband but did not care to do so until she had arranged for the care of the children. In her letter she charged me most particularly not to permit them to tease you, declaring that she was already imposing quite sufficiently upon your good nature by permitting you to house them and that it would be quite too bad if they were also to cut up your peace."

"Then you are not, I take it, acquainted with your charges?" said his lordship grimly.

"No, milord."

"I trust that they will not give you cause to repent your rashness in accepting a post of which you knew so little. It is only fair to warn you that you will have your hands full. In addition to my sister's three, the schoolroom party includes my nephew Benedict, my younger brother's only child. His parents died during an outbreak of cholera and he was left to my guardianship. Strictly speaking, the charge of one who can only be described as a young rapscallion is no part of your duties, since he has his own tutor. But you will soon discover that he exerts a good deal of influence over your pupils, especially the two younger ones, so that in self defence you will find it necessary to make him mind you. Let me assure you of my entire support in any measures that you may judge necessary to suppress his genius for leading his cousins into mischief. In fact it might be better if you leave his punishment in my hands, or just report him to his tutor if he gets up to any of his tricks."

The big blue-grey eyes regarded him solemnly. "How old is your nephew, milord?"

"He will be thirteen next month."

The lady nodded sagely. "Then if I am for ever telling tales of him I shall entirely forfeit his respect. Deservedly, too. I think it will be better if I use my own methods of discipline. I am not without experience. Apart from my pupils, I have brothers of my own. I do not despair of establishing good relations with your nephew."

His lordship bowed. "As you wish, ma'am. But do not allow professional pride to deter you from claiming my support if you feel that it is needed."

She gave him a quaint little half-nod, half-bow of assent, and rose as the maid came into the library to show her to her room. At least she had some spirit behind the unattractive façade, decided by his lordship, revising his opinion rather more favourably at this assertion of independence. It would be interesting to see what she made of young Benedict. If she mastered that young scapegrace she would certainly be worthy of his guardian's deepest respect! The boy was spoiled, he supposed ruefully. Delicate health in childhood had caused him to be educated at home, and sympathy for his orphaned state, combined with natural affection aroused by a lively and engaging personality had made him very much the darling of the household. Nor, as an only child, had his full propensities for mischief been displayed. It was not until his cousins had come to spend the summer at Valminster that he began to demonstrate qualities of leadership and organisation that would stand him in good stead in later life if, as he probably would, he should choose to follow his father into the army.

On the domestic front these qualities were less appreciated. A number of Master Benedict's whilom supporters discovered that he had long outgrown his youthful delicacy and was now capable of plaguing the lives out of them. His sunny good humour and his readiness to accept defeat in good part when he found himself out-generalled, ensured a high degree of tolerance from servants who had known him from his cradle, but as his guardian, the Earl had felt that he was in a fair way to becoming thoroughly out of hand. He supposed that he ought to make more effort to exert his own authority since he suspected that the boy could twist his tutor round his

finger. School discipline would bear harshly
on him if he was permitted to set authority
at defiance in his present outrageous fashion,
yet it seemed a pity to cramp his freedom
during what would be, to all intents and pur-
poses, the last summer of his childhood. By
next year school would have set its mark on
him. Next summer, too, there would be no
family of cousins to initiate him into the give
and take that would help him to settle into
school life. The Earl decided to hold his hand
a little longer, but to keep a closer watch upon
the activities of the schoolroom party in general and upon Master Benedict in particular.

Having supervised the process of unpack-
ing her simple belongings, bestowing most of
them in drawers and cupboards with her own
hands (which caused the handmaiden who
waited upon her to report that, 'Miss seemed
to be a pleasant sort of lady, not one of the
proud kind, even if she wasn't much to look
at'), Miss Graine Ashley devoted herself to
a careful inspection of the rooms that had
been allotted to her.

She was very pleasantly surprised. She had
been fortunate, she decided. It was a pity that
she must reside in a masculine household,
but she had taken her own measures to coun-
teract the discomforts of that particular situation, and certainly the accommodation provided was far superior to anything that she

had encountered in her previous posts. In fact she would have supposed the comfortable bedroom and sitting room to have been guest chambers, so pleasant and attractively furnished as they were. Moreover she had been treated with perfect respect by such servants as she had had dealings with. To one who was well accustomed to treading the difficult path of the governess who was neither gentry nor servant but an employee who must establish her own claim to gentility, this was a significant pointer. In her experience, good servants and good employers went together. She thought the better of the Earl because his butler had shown her proper deference and his housemaid had smiled in friendly fashion as she performed her duties. It was not unusual for servants who were obliged to wait on so ignoble a being as a governess to be sullen and covertly insolent. Miss Ashley was inclined to view her immediate future hopefully, despite the warning that she had received from his lordship. Remembering some of her experiences—in particular some of the exploits of her brothers—she felt that she was well prepared for most of the tricks that a twelve-year-old schoolboy was likely to try. It was a pity that circumstances compelled her to play a part. It would all have been very much simpler if she could just have been her natural self. Much would depend, of course,

on the personality of the sinner. But she had
a good deal of faith in her own capabilities,
and it would give her considerable satisfaction to prove them to that cool, doubting
Thomas who had dismissed her so kindly
from his presence. Not that his name *was*
Thomas. It was something rather outlandish
which she could not at the moment recall,
and no business of hers in any case.

She took another look at the contents of
her wardrobe. Certainly nothing sufficiently
glamorous to cause a maid to pry, she thought,
with a humorous little grimace that would
have surprised the Earl. But one could not
be too careful. The charming little escritoire
that had been provided for her use had a
drawer that could be locked. She studied her
face critically in the mirror, decided that for
the moment no repairs were needed, and bestowed the sticks of grease paint and several
boxes and packages in the drawer, carefully
locking it and putting the key on a ribbon
that she hung round her neck. A final inspection assured her that the shifts with the
padded shoulders were modestly folded away
in the middle of a pile of under-linen. It was
going to be a great nuisance to maintain her
disguise, simple as it was, with so many other
things to think about. But she was already
committed and now she must go through with
it. Even if, in face of her impersonal reception

from her nominal employer, it no longer seemed so necessary.

She shrugged, wondered what her pupils were doing and when she would meet them, and settled down to write a letter to her sister Bridget to announce her safe arrival. Perhaps the Earl would be willing to frank it for her.

She met her eldest charge, the sixteen-year-old Beatrice, at dinner that night. The girl explained that she and Benedict were permitted to dine with the grown-ups unless guests were expected. Mr Read, Benedict's tutor, was also of the party. Benedict himself had been denied the treat, having been sentenced to bread and milk in the schoolroom. If he showed no more sense than a babe in the nursery, he must expect to be treated like one, pronounced the Earl. It emerged that his lordship had come upon the three youngsters playing a game called 'Astleys', Benedict standing on his hands on the pony's back while Bridget led it round the paddock, and explaining to his juniors, though rather breathlessly, how to maintain this feat of balance. His uncle had been just in time to stop the eight-year-old Adam from attempting to emulate this exploit, Bridget having regretfully declined a polite invitation to take first turn because the feat was one that was difficult to perform when hampered by petticoats.

Graine listened to this account with an unmoved countenance, though her self control was sorely tried. She was divided between amusement and relief. This sort of thing she could deal with. Reckless and ill-judged, of course, since the younger children might easily have been injured, but not sly or malicious. She began to look forward to her encounters with Master Benedict, though she could not help regretting that the 'Astleys' episode had been ill-timed from her point of view. The culprit had been made to look small in the eyes of the new governess before they had even met. It would do nothing to dispose him in her favour.

In fact she had no trouble at all for the better part of a week. The Browning children posed no problems. Beatrice, who would make her debut next year, loved pretty clothes and talked eagerly of all the things she would do when she was launched into Society, but was still something of a tomboy. Graine liked her unaffected manners and thought she showed promise of being as great a success as her Mama. The two younger ones, Bridget named for Graine's sister and Adam, the Brownings' cherished only son, were normal likeable youngsters, easily led but equally easily controlled. In the intimate atmosphere of the schoolroom she ventured to lower her guard a little and allow her natural vivacity to peep out. Her pupils tended to like her. She made lessons interesting and was not above bending the rules occasionally on a fine day. A great many lessons could be done satisfactorily out of doors. Though it was a pity, thought the Brownings, that Miss Ashley did not enter fully into their enthusiasm for outdoor pursuits. Perhaps one would not expect a governess to care for swimming (thus Beatrice) but surely boating on the lake was perfectly proper, and Uncle Ross would not permit them to go unless Miss Ashley and Mr Read both accompanied them. While as for riding and driving, one might almost think that the newcomer was afraid of horses. Such a person might win tolerance. She could never win respect or affection.

Graine came into the schoolroom one morning after breakfast to find three heads bent studiously over their tasks. That in itself was enough to arouse her suspicions, and the presence of Benedict, who should have been engaged with Mr Read in the library, did nothing to allay them. Moreover he apologised so politely for his intrusion that it was abundantly plain that there was something in the wind.

"Mr Read said I might attempt the still life group that you set up for Beatrice yesterday," he said glibly. "I'll be mum as a mouse, I promise."

For some reason this remark struck Bridget as being irresistibly funny. She erupted into giggles, to be sternly frowned down by her cousin. "Miss Ashley won't permit me to stay if you are going to make such a fuss," he told her, in so severe a voice that she was instantly quelled.

Graine gave the required permission and lessons proceeded decorously enough for some twenty minutes, though neither Bridget nor Adam appeared to derive much profit from them. Adam's thoughts seemed to be on other things and Bridget was still in a state of suppressed giggles. Adam's struggles with the nine times table brought matters to a head. He managed quite confidently as far as four nines, but five produced a long pause until he suddenly said, in an oddly shaky little voice, "Miss Ashley, do you know there's a mouse on your skirt?"

Graine glanced down. Sure enough there was a small white mouse ensconced in the modest ruffle that edged her plain gown, sitting up on his hind legs and gazing about him warily, mouse fashion, with tiny darting movements. She had to acknowledge a degree of defeat, for Benedict had succeeded in placing him there without attracting her attention even though she had been on the alert for mischief.

"Oh, the dear little fellow," she said pleasantly. "Just look at him! Not a bit afraid. You must move very gently, children, so as not to startle him. Is he yours, Benedict? Is he tame enough to come to you if you offer him food? A few crumbs of biscuit might tempt him if he knows you well enough. But you should shut him up more securely," she reproved gently. "Mice are such sensitive little creatures. At large among a crowd of people who must appear monstrous in his sight, he might have been terrified to the point of panic. I hope you will not mind my giving you a hint on this head. My brothers and I kept all kinds of pets, and mice were among my particular favourites."

Two

She gained some prestige from this encounter, and several casually dropped anecdotes about her childhood and the pets that had enlivened it did something to put her stock higher. She took the precaution of dwelling rapturously on the beauty of a grass snake that her brother Dominic had cherished, since she could not rely on her ability to sustain a calm front if any of her charges introduced one of the horrid slithery reptiles into the room. Frogs and toads, newts, guinea pigs and all the usual domestic pets, but not even her brothers had been able to cure her of her aversion to snakes. But on the whole she doubted if they would try the same sort of trick again. His lordship had said that Benedict was full of ingenious ideas. She wondered what he would try next.

Ingenious he might be, but he lacked patience. He had not the cunning to wait until she might be regarded as being lulled into a sense of false security. He *did* wait until Beatrice was absent. Beatrice was beginning to think herself too old for childish pranks, and what was more, Miss Ashley had won her over to a certain extent by telling her something of the delights that she would enjoy when she made her début next year. Bea was not likely to approve of the time honoured practice of spreading glue on the governess's chair. She was more likely to protest that it was a mean trick to play, even if it did make the poor woman lookly uncommonly foolish. In fact Benedict himself was rather ashamed of it. It was not very original. But what were you to do with a woman who raised no objection to mice running over her skirts?

He picked his time carefully. Bea had been dispatched in charge of one of the abigails to call upon her godmother. Miss Ashley had taken the two younger children for a ramble in the home wood and his lordship had invited Mr Read to give his opinion on a new pony that he had just bought for Adam. Benedict was also invited to be of this party, but he could look at Adam's pony any time. Such an opportunity for mischief might not occur again. It took only a few minutes to purloin the glue pot from the carpenter's shop, spread a thin film of glue on the chair that Miss Ashley always occupied at the head of the table and return the pot to its proper place. His only fear was that the little party might loiter over their ramble so that the glue would have time to harden before they arrived. But all went well. He had just time to settle himself in the window-seat with a book—in itself an occupation likely to arouse the deepest suspicion in a wary soul—when he heard sounds of arrival.

Graine would have fallen into the trap if it had not been for the butterfly. The room was empty, Benedict having decided that he had time to make good his escape. It was wiser not to linger on the scene of one's crimes, however great the temptation to watch the success of one's scheming. Having sent the children to wash their hands for tea and tidied her own person, she was strolling lazily across to her usual chair when she noticed the hapless insect, a large cabbage white, perched on the seat of her chair and struggling ineffectually to rise. It was easy enough to see what had happened. No doubt some constituent of the glue had attracted the wretched creature to its doom. Graine did not hesitate. She killed it with one sharp blow and dropped the frail dust that remained out of the open window. She was not sentimental about such matters, save to decide that this time Master Benedict should not escape scot-free. A tongue lashing at least he deserved for his heedlessness. But first to establish a superior tactical position. Swiftly she disposed herself in Benedict's usual seat and thanked the gods of chance when Adam and Bridget, sharp-set after their excursion, came racing in demanding sustenance. Placidly she poured milk, passed bread and butter and cake and drew attention to the special treat of a dish of hot muffins which were great favourites.

She greeted Benedict's belated arrival with a light apology for having usurped his usual chair. "But it is cooler here, you see, and I was so hot after our exertions. You will not mind sitting at the head of the table for once."

Benedict minded very much. He said that he was not hungry—which was a downright lie, with the delicious scent of those muffins making his mouth water—and wandered about the room in a disconsolate fashion which afforded Miss Ashley considerable satisfaction. She waited until Adam and Bridget had finished their meal and gone off to watch the feeding of a litter of puppies at the gardener's cottage. Uncle Ross had rashly promised that they should have one for themselves, and they were still earnestly debating the choice. As the door closed behind them she said directly, "I am waiting for your apology, Benedict. You will scarcely deny your responsibility. None of the others had the opportunity."

He was unprepared for the swiftness of the attack. She had always seemed so mild, even timid. His chin went up defiantly and he sounded almost comically like his uncle as he said, "I am not in the habit of permitting others to take the blame for my misdeeds. Yes, I am responsible. And I will say I am sorry, but not for putting glue on the chair. Only for the miscarriage of my plan."

Graine eyed him steadily. "That is insolence," she said quietly. "You would be well served if I reported you to Mr Read. I shall not do so, however. I will ask you rather to consider the results of your infantile prank if it had succeeded. You would have made me look foolish for a moment or two, until I realised what had happened. Very amusing, I make no doubt. But I do not think you are really heartless or cruel. If *you* had sat on that chair, your parents or your uncle would have bought you a new pair of breeches and the whole thing would have been forgotten in a week. A governess in my position can afford perhaps one new gown in a year. The one I am wearing is almost new, and I would expect it to last me three or four years at least. It would have been ruined beyond repair. Is that what you intended?"

He flushed and looked down, drawing patterns on the carpet with one toe and muttering something to the effect that he had not thought about that. Then he fell silent for a moment, trying to comprehend the feelings of someone who had to count the cost of spoiled clothing. Eventually he looked up at Graine with the smile that had endeared him even to his victims.

"If I didn't say I was sorry, I can at least say that I am truly glad your gown was not spoiled. And it *was* an infantile prank." His normal mischievous grin dawned. "I'll think of something much better next time," he promised cheerfully, "and it's decent of you not to report me to Mr Read. His idea of a punishment is to make me learn miles and miles of Latin verse, and in this weather it's downright sinful to be stewing indoors over stuffy books. Thank you."

So the battle was not quite won. Probably that reference to an infantile prank had stung rather more than she had intended. But she reckoned she was making good progress, and wondered, with amused interest, what form the next trial of strength would take.

It proved to be another hoary relic—the

haunted gallery. But this time she could at
least admire the artistry with which it was
performed. The actor-manager showed no impatience. He was getting his adversary's
measure, realising that she was not to be
stampeded into panic without good cause. If
he could only get the better of her once, she
thought, he would probably be satisfied, for
in the ordinary way relations between them
were cordial enough. More than ready for
school, she grimaced. An active body and a
fertile brain and no outlet for his excess ener-
gies. At the moment she was his chosen tar-
get, and since their last encounter she was
quite prepared to believe that there was no
malice in his dealings. It was simply that
she presented a problem that he wanted to
solve.

His story of the haunted gallery—she
checked it in the library records—was the
purest fabrication. It concerned the Countess
of Queen Elizabeth's day whose husband, following the pattern of so many of that sov-
ereign's subjects, had gone sea-faring. Unfortunately he had died at sea of some pestilent
fever. According to Benedict's version of the
legend, his wife had been instantly aware of
her husband's decease, even though the actual news had not reached her for the better
part of a year. She had donned widow's garb
and mourned him as dead from that day.

Now, on the anniversary of his death, she walked up and down the long gallery, wailing and wringing her hands. She would, of course, thought Graine, hiding her amusement behind a mask of respectful attention. So far as she could judge the two younger children were not in the plot. Their awed fascination as they listened was unfeigned. But there was a certain conscious look in Beatrice's eyes. Was she destined to play the part of the unhappy Countess, wondered her duenna? She was just young enough, just sufficiently a scapegrace still, to succumb to such a temptation.

A whole week passed and nothing further transpired. Referring casually to the legend, Graine was informed by its originator that on certain occasions the Tudor Earl also haunted his former home. Presumably he was permitted to do so in an attempt to console his unhappy wife, for the pair were heard in conversation. But at this point Benedict's invention failed him sadly. Perhaps it was asking too much of a lad not yet in his teens to devise a convincing conversation for the reunited pair. The Earl, he reported, when pressed for further details, had been heard to enquire after his favourite horse, and for someone called Rollo, who was thought to be one of his hounds.

"Not for his children?" asked Graine, sounding much shocked.

Benedict hastily disposed of the offspring of his mythical pair. "They had no children," he told her triumphantly. "That was what made it so sad, you see. Because of the succession," he added largely.

Graine accepted this with due sympathy but could not resist probing just a little further. "And the Countess?" she urged. "Does she answer him?"

"Well I expect she tells him about the horse and the dog, but you can't really tell what she says because her voice is all weepy," decided the harrassed inventor. But here he caught a meaning glance from his Cousin Beatrice which clearly threatened the withdrawal of her support if she were not given a proper speaking part in this dramatic piece. He forced himself to a final creative effort.

"Oh yes! She asks him what he has brought her back from the Spanish Main," he concluded thankfully.

Graine made the excuse of seeing that Bridget and Adam were safely in bed and the candles out, and escaped from the room before her giggles overcame her. She felt that she could hardly wait for the opening night of this historic drama, and wished that she was on sufficiently intimate terms with Mr Read or even with his lordship to be able to share the joke. But Mr Read was a sober-minded young man, upright and conscientious but sadly deficient in sense of humour, while his lordship, though always pleasant and courteous when they chanced to meet, was too far removed from her humble orbit.

The site for the haunting had been well chosen, since Graine's rooms opened on to the long gallery. The wailing noise that signalled the rise of the curtain was certainly emitted by a remarkably healthy ghost. Graine shook her head sadly. Evidently Beatrice was not gifted with dramatic sensitivity. But perhaps she should be forgiven, since she was also charged with the task of attracting the required audience. Dutifully Graine picked up her candle and went out into the gallery.

The lamp which normally illuminated the far end of the gallery had been extinguished, in itself an unusual circumstance. But perhaps the Valminster ghosts did not like bright lights. It was really rather a pity, because they were beautifully dressed in the costume of Elizabeth's day, the lady in widespreading farthingale, the gentleman in doublet and padded breeches. A purist might have suggested that the gentleman should not have been wearing a mask, while the floating veil that covered the lady's head and face was equally out of keeping, though she made great play with it, crushing it between her fingers and almost rending it apart in her anguish. The conversation between the pair closely followed the lines that Benedict had laid down, but there was one surprise. When asked by his wife what pretty gauds he had brought for her, the gentleman favoured her with a courtly bow, offered her his arm and invited her to come with him and see for herself. Unfortunately Graine sneezed at that very moment, though luckily the candle flame only flickered and did not go out. But by the time it steadied again, the ghostly pair had vanished.

For a moment she could not believe her eyes. Certainly they had not passed her, and there could not have been time for them to have reached the other end of the gallery. There must be some concealed doorway with which the children were probably familiar. It was not a thought that she cared for. Practical jokes were all very well and certainly she had got a good deal of amusement out of this one, but the thought of a concealed entrance by which any one could gain access to the gallery was a different matter. However she did not propose to lose sleep over it. No harm had befallen her during the weeks she had spent at the castle. It was unlikely to do so tonight. She would take the added precaution of locking her bedroom door and she would speak to Bosworth about it in the morning.

She dispatched the schoolroom maid with a message for that dignitary as soon as the children's breakfast had been served. "Ask him if he will wait upon me at some convenient time," she said. "The matter is not urgent."

Beatrice and Benedict exchanged glances and applied themselves to their breakfasts with unusual singlemindedness. The summons to Bosworth might have nothing to do with last night's little escapade, but they could not be wholly at ease. They had been waiting for Miss Ashley to make some reference to the visitation that she had observed last night, half anxious, half wishing that she would. Actually the whole thing had fallen rather flat. Miss Ashley had neither screamed nor run. Instead she had advanced towards them steadily, candle in hand. They had been quite thankful for that fortuitous sneeze that had given them time to slip into the priest's hole and lie hid until they heard her bedroom door close.

Bosworth had taken a liking to Miss Ashley. She might not be much to look at but she had a pleasant way with her. The message that she had sent proved his point. She had not sent for him. She had asked him to wait upon her. Therefore, as he explained to his

crony, Mrs Palmer, he would not keep her
waiting in order to establish his own importance in the hierarchy, but would do so at
once.

"And while you're about it you might ask
her what those children have been up to in
the attics," snorted Mrs Palmer. "Maria was
up there this morning and she says it looks
like a rag fair. They've been into all the old
chests, dragging out finery that's been stored
away for generations. Playing at dressing up,
I suppose, and harmless enough compared
with some of the games that Master Benedict
puts them up to. But what I says is that they
should put things away orderly when they've
done with them. There's silks and velvets and
such-like laid away up there, some of them
sewn with jewels, too. They should be taught
to value them, not just toss them aside when
they weary of playing with them. Let alone
the maids have plenty enough to do without
running around waiting on careless children.
They seem to mind Miss Ashley pretty well.
Get her to have a word with them."

Bosworth nodded majestic assent to these
views and departed to the schoolroom. Miss
Ashley gave him a polite good morning and
thanked him for attending to her request so
promptly.

"It is probably nothing," she said apologetically, "but I thought you were the proper

person to advise me. Last night some unusual noise disturbed me. I went out into the gallery to investigate. The lamp had gone out, but by the light of my candle I saw someone or something disappear *through* the panelling. Pray accept my assurance that I am *not* a fanciful person, and tell me, is there any concealed doorway or secret room in that part of the gallery?"

"Yes, miss, there is," returned Bosworth readily. "There's the priest's hole. I thought you would know of it. Master Benedict can show you the trick. It's simple enough. It's just a tiny room behind the panelling where they used to hide the priests in the bad old days when to be a Roman Catholic might take you to Smithfield to be burned at the stake. But there's only the one way in. Nobody could get into the house from outside by using it. What sort of noises did you hear?"

"It's difficult to say," said Graine, with some degree of truth. "Footsteps. Voices. You know how it is when you are awakened from sleep. You can never be sure what roused you. But now that I know there is no danger of housebreakers I shall not give the matter another thought."

Bosworth looked unconvinced, and his glanced flickered in a speculative way to Benedict, but that young man preserved an innocent front. The butler accepted defeat.

"Then if I may make so bold, miss, Mrs Palmer asks if you would have a word with the young ladies and gentlemen about the state of the attics. Seems they'd been looking through some of the things that were stored away up there and had left them in a fine old state."

That solved one little bit of puzzle, decided Miss Ashley, as she assured Bosworth that all should be put in order and asked him to give her apologies to Mrs Palmer. She had wondered how they had contrived those costumes.

She poured herself another cup of coffee while she meditated the best way of intimating to the culprits that she was perfectly well aware of their identities. Young Bridget intervened.

"Weren't you frightened, Miss Ashley? When you heard noises in the night? I'm sure I would never be brave enough to get up and go to see who it was. I should put my head under the bedclothes and hope it would go away."

"Didn't you think that perhaps it was ghosts?" demanded Benedict boldly. "It might have been the Tudor Earl and his Countess."

"They would not frighten me nearly so much as housebreakers," Graine told him. "As a child I spent long holidays with an aunt who occupied a Grace and Favour apartment at Hampton Court. The Silver Stick Gallery, it was called. And at Hampton Court, you must know, there are so many ghosts that one grows quite accustomed. The ghost of Queen Jane Seymour walks in the Clock Court. She carries a lighted candle with a flame that never flickers. And there is the ghost of Queen Katharine Howard, of course, as well as that of Dame Sybil Penn who was foster mother to the little King Edward. But I never heard of them doing any one any harm, whereas a housebreaker might behave very violently indeed if interrupted in his nefarious ways. The voices that I heard last night could well have been Valminster voices. They had a very familiar ring. But I had no cause to be afraid of them. If they were ghost voices they were family ghosts going about their own business. If the noises were made by humans, then I can only hope that they don't choose the long gallery to play their tricks on another occasion. To have one's sleep disturbed for no good reason is apt to make one very cross."

Benedict looked her straight in the eye. "You knew all the time that it was us. Don't be too cross with Bea. I talked her into it, and she only agreed because she loves dressing up. It was my idea. Bea said all along that you wouldn't be taken in, but I thought that with the lamp out—"

At which singularly inauspicious moment there came a tap at the door and the Earl walked in.

He bade the little group good morning, wondering what had caused the guilty expressions worn by the three senior members of the party, for Graine was quite as much taken aback as the two sinners, and said easily, "And what sort of a report does Miss Ashley give of her pupils this morning? Mr Read assures me that Benedict has been quite impossibly virtuous for three whole days. It seemed to me that such unprecedented behaviour should be suitably rewarded. There is a fair in the village this week. Beatrice is a little old for such rustic joys, but perhaps for once she can forget her advanced age. What do you say, Miss Ashley? If you are ready to give these pestiferous brats a clean bill, I am willing to lend my escort."

Well—he had certainly offered to support her attempts at discipline, and he could scarcely have put a stronger weapon into her hands. The dismay on Benedict's face was really quite pitiful. She guessed that this was a treat long desired. She said briskly, "If by a clean bill you are to understand that all your nephews and nieces are positive pattern cards of virtue, then, no, they are not. If, on the other hand you wish to know if they are amenable to discipline and are quite as virtuous as healthy children have any right to be, then, yes, they are. I think I may say that we are good friends and rub along very comfortably together. On the whole I think they deserve a treat," she concluded, and had her reward in the ring of brightening faces.

Having decided that they would lunch early so that they could spend the whole afternoon enjoying such delights as the penny peepshow, a conjurer who could swallow fire and also conjure rings off ladies' fingers only to find them again in gentlemen's pockets and a monkey who could walk a tight-rope carrying a basket of eggs and turn head over heels without breaking them, they agreed that the younger members of the party should travel in the pony cart with a groom in charge, while Miss Ashley and Beatrice would go with the Earl in the carriage, and his lordship took his leave.

Benedict said soberly, "Miss Ashley, you're a regular trump. We don't deserve it—at least *I* don't—but I truly, truly thank you. I can't promise never to tease you again, because the things I do often seem to tease grown-ups when I didn't mean to. But I will try very hard to think first. About things like spoiling your dress and not waking you up when you are tired." And then, this unaccustomed sobriety yielding to his natural resilience, "And some day, when there's nothing much to do, will you tell us all about the ghosts at Hampton Court?"

Three

Vaguely the Earl had been aware that a certain degree of domestic peace had descended upon his establishment. The children seemed less unruly, though no one could say that they were unnaturally subdued. There were fewer complaints from the servants about Master Benedict's misdeeds. In his innocence he had supposed that they were settling down together and finding satisfactory entertainment in each other's society, which gave their elders a much more peaceful existence. Rather smugly he reflected that he had always been an advocate of large families, believing that they were a good preparation for the rough and tumble that life probably held in store.

It did not occur to him that, still a bachelor at thirty seven and with no particular interest in the opposite sex, he was not allowing a great deal of time for putting his theories into practice. It was satisfactory, though, that his nephews and nieces should provide such a striking example. Benedict, for instance, was becoming positively civilised. Since his lordship was driving the carriage himself, it was pretty to see the boy hand Miss Ashley and Beatrice up without a trace of self-consciousness before turning away to his own humbler vehicle. One didn't want a boy to be too soft, but there was something to be said for the refining effects of petticoat influence. He smiled benignly upon his nieces.

The only incident that threatened to mar the harmony of the afternoon was Beatrice's desire to have her fortune told and her uncle's disapproval. In his view, fortune tellers were charlatans, preying on the credulous. Bea should have more sense than to listen to their fabrications. Tumblers, jugglers, performing animals were skilled entertainers. Let her take her pleasure in watching them. He brushed past the lad who was standing outside the fortune teller's booth, assuring prospective customers that the soothsayer, his grandmother, was of true Romany blood; was, indeed, a queen among her own people. Certainly there was a strong tincture of gypsy blood visible in the boy's own colouring and in his supple grace of movement. The Valminster party, under the stern guidance of their mentor, resisted his inviting gestures and moved on relentlessly, despite Beatrice's backward glances. His lordship was able once more to resume his reflections upon the beneficial effects of daily association with the female sex. But an afternoon spent in sampling all the delights of the fair raised considerable doubt in his mind as to the precise source of the petticoat influence that had exercised such an admirable effect on Benedict. To be sure the boy picked up Bridget when she tripped and fell, but he brushed her down in very cursory fashion, assured her that she wasn't really hurt and bade her stop bawling in a most unchivalrous way. Perhaps Bridget, so close to him in age, did not strike him as a creature to be cherished and protected. It was not until they had made the whole round of the offered attractions and Miss Ashley had gently but firmly rejected Adam's plea for just one more ride on the whirligig, that the truth began to dawn on him.

"Fairings!" exclaimed Benedict. "We haven't bought any fairings."

The choice was fairly limited. Luckily Adam was easily contented with a jack-in-the-box and Bridget enraptured by a string of varicoloured beads. Beatrice chose a scarf which her Mama would undoubtedly have stigmatized as gaudy, but after her earlier disappointment Graine had not the heart to deny her. Benedict vanished for ten minutes to return stuffing several small packets into his pockets and offering no account of their contents.

His lordship suggested that they should repair to the inn where they had left the carriages and partake of suitable refreshment before they undertook the rigours of the return journey, but Benedict said indignantly, "But we have no fairing for Miss Ashley."

Nothing would serve but that he should embark on a search forthwith. The others might proceed to the Swan and Pigeons. He would join them as soon as he had procured an appropriate token.

In fact he was not long, arriving with his face brimming with mischief and begging Miss Ashley to open the small parcel right away.

It contained a pink sugar mouse with a white string tail.

"You said you liked mice," said Benedict with a twinkle. "I'm sorry they had no white ones."

Miss Ashley chuckled; the children laughed; only his lordship was puzzled by what seemed to him an odd choice of gift. A handkerchief, now, or even a brooch would have been well within the boy's means.

Miss Ashley took pity on his puzzled expression. "We were talking about the pets that my brothers and I kept when we were children," she told him kindly, "and I mentioned my partiality for white mice. Thank you very much, Benedict. Only I shall not want to eat it, you know, any more than I could eat rabbit pie after I had fed and fondled the poor little creatures that went to its making."

The Earl could see no similarity between the two cases, but he was more concerned to consider this new aspect of Miss Ashley's relationship with Benedict. To be sure the young woman was rather more forthcoming than she had been at their first meeting, but he still found it surprising that she had so easily established some sort of understanding with his difficult nephew. He had no illusions where Benedict was concerned and had a pretty adequate notion of the means that the boy had used to dispose of the several tutors who had preceded Mr Read. Now he actually wondered if Miss Ashley's presence in his household accounted for the fact that Mr Read had lasted so long. But why? No doubt she had all the virtues and a well-informed mind, but those qualities had never appealed to Benedict before her arrival.

Benedict himself could not have enlightened him. He could not have said when or why he had begun to like Miss Ashley. Hard pressed he might have muttered that she was a good plucked 'un, or even that she played fair. But that was not quite all. Benedict felt that there was more to Miss Ashley than met the eye. He was an observant youth and it had struck him that Miss Ashley's awkward halting gait was miraculously cured if ever she was required to move quickly. He had noticed it again this very afternoon when Bridget had tumbled. Miss Ashley had fallen behind with Adam, but she had been there in a flash when she was needed. Benedict suspected that she could run like a deer. So why should she pretend? He scented a mystery and found it intriguing. Innate good breeding told him that he should not seek to pry into Miss Ashley's secrets, but there could be no harm in just noticing things, could there?

Miss Ashley had indeed grown rather lax in her routine of disguise. As the weather grew warmer she heartily wished that she had never embarked on a career of deceit, especially as it had proved to be totally unnecessary. In fact, she thought, unwillingly applying a layer of grease paint to a petal-smooth skin, it began to look as though she had vastly over-rated her personal attractions. The thing was that she had been obliged to resign two otherwise desirable posts in order to evade masculine attentions that amounted almost to persecution. In the first case the son of the house, a stripling of seventeen, had dangled after her in a fashion that embarrassed not only his lady love but his parents. They had been kind and fair, realising that it was not her fault, that she had given him no encouragement. But the more she snubbed him, the more he yearned, and there was nothing for it but to leave. She had moved on to take charge of two young children, thinking to avoid dealings with callow youths, but in the next establishment it was the guests who posed the problem. They— or several of them—seemed to think that a pretty governess was provided for *their* entertainment. Mostly there was no harm in them, but Graine found their gallantries embarrassing. When the lady of the house began to display a degree of jealousy, it was obviously time to move on again.

That was when her sister had suggested the possibility of a post with the Brownings. A temporary post at present. Sir John was going to Copenhagen and his wife wished to go with him. But whether the children would eventually join their parents, or whether Lady Elizabeth would open up Mounsell Park, their country home, was not yet de-

cided. In either case Graine hoped that she
would be kept on. She liked the children and
could settle herself very happily in the country, while the possibility of foreign travel was
also appealing. Unaware of the eagle eye that
Benedict was exercising over her proceed-
ings, and of a further complication that was
about to descend upon her, she touched the
sugar mouse with a gentle fore-finger and
then busied herself in applying the brown
velvet patch that simulated the mole on the
side of her nose. There had been no need for
these disfiguring additions in *this* household,
she thought ruefully, and the caps beneath
which she had hidden her pretty hair made
her head feel hot and heavy. She sighed,
locked away grease paint and patch box, and
went down to dinner. For the first time it
struck her that she might have to keep up
the pretence for months, perhaps years. It
was a depressing thought. Her sister Bridget
(who knew nothing of her present masquerade) had frequently scolded her for embark-
ing on ill-judged activities without thinking
far enough ahead. This was a case in point.
But at least, she comforted herself, her dis-
ciplinary difficulties with her pupils were in
a fair way to being solved.

They were all in the home paddock next
day watching young Adam school his new
pony over the series of low obstacles that had

been set up for his especial benefit, when one of the footmen came from the house with a message for Miss Ashley.

"A gentleman to see you, miss. Your brother, he says, and it's urgent. So his lordship told me to stay here and keep an eye on the young ladies and gentlemen while you go to attend to it."

His delighted face showed that the task was much to his liking. Graine hid a sympathetic grin. Henry was not very old, Bosworth a strict taskmaster. She could well understand that half an hour out of doors in the easy-going atmosphere of the schoolroom world was an acceptable release from his usual duties. But what in the world could Dominic be wanting with her? And how had he got leave from school to make the journey?

When her father's untimely death in the hunting field had disclosed the shocking state to which rash speculation and sheer ill-luck with the blood stock in which he had invested his money had reduced Hugh Ashley's fortune, Dominic's godfather had come to the rescue so far as the boy was concerned. He should live in town with Sir Everard and attend Westminster School as a day pupil. Even the holidays need not present much difficulty. Sir Everard, who was some kind of a distant cousin as well as godfather, had a small place of his own in Ireland where he often spent the summer. Dominic could go with him if it happened to be inconvenient for him to stay with his sister Bridget and her husband. Dominic had brightened considerably at this suggestion. Accustomed to the casual, friendly ways of a shabby, run-down but very contented Irish holding, he had small fancy for the restrictions of Town life. He knew that he must get a good education, for he would have his own way to make in the world, but Town life and school would be endurable if one could look forward to holidays in Ireland.

It was the threat to his summer holiday that had brought him hurrying to his sister for support, as she learned even before he greeted her. Henry had said that he had left the young gentleman talking with his lord-ship in the library. As Graine went in she heard her brother exclaiming indignantly, "There could be no enduring it. Rome! At the height of the summer. And with Uncle Everard it would be all stuffy churches and picture galleries. Not even jolly things like the Colosseum and the Catacombs. And the dreadful part of it is that he thinks he's giving me a high treat and keeps prosing on about ancient cultures and artistic opportunities which I don't care a straw about."

At this point in his diatribe he became aware that his sister had entered the room and rose to greet her. Lord Valminster, who had been listening with sympathetic interest, could not fail to notice his startled expression, for his mouth dropped open and his eyebrows shot up in quite unmistakeable fashion. He turned to look at Miss Ashley to see what had so discomposed her brother. She looked strained and anxious and she was holding out her hands in a very peculiar fashion, the right wrist supported in the left hand, the right thumb and first finger linked to form a circle. He was just about to enquire if she had hurt her hand when he noticed that the hand her brother extended in greeting was shaping a similar circle. A swift glance at the boy's face surprised a mischievous grin which had temporarily banished the aggrieved expression. His lordship realised that he had been privileged to witness some private form of communication by which members of the Ashley family exchanged messages. So far as he could remember from the days of his own youth, such signs were generally a warning against accidental betrayal. He wondered what guilty secret Miss Ashley was guarding so anxiously. Her brother's prompt response seemed to have reassured her, for she was now addressing him with a vivacity that his lordship had not seen in her before, in one breath expressing her delight at seeing him, in the next asking if he had leave from school and scolding him for taking up Lord Valminster's time with his troubles.

His lordship rose. "As to that, Miss Ashley, it is I who should apologise for intruding upon what you would doubtless prefer to be a private interview. However, before I leave you I have a suggestion to make. Your brother can perfectly well spend his holiday here. I am a little acquainted with Sir Everard Hastings. In fact I share a good many of his antiquarian and artistic tastes"—this with a gleam of laughter in his eyes for the abashed Dominic—"and I think if I were to put it to him that his Roman tour would be far more enjoyable without the society of a restless schoolboy bored to the point of sullenness, he might be persuaded to consent to such a scheme. Your brother—Dominic, is it—is far too young for large doses of culture. He would do better here. It may not be Ireland, but at least he can follow his natural bent for country living. Nor need either of you think yourselves indebted to me. Your sister will tell you, Dominic, that I have a young nephew who will be all the better for the company of an older boy who shares his interests and can possibly restrain some of his less orthodox activities. He is to go to school next half, and I daresay you could give him some useful hints that may serve to keep him out of trouble at least with his contemporaries. I will leave you to talk it over with your sister, and if you think well of the suggestion I will have a word with Sir Everard."

A little dazed by this sudden prospect of release from a tour that would be nothing but a penance, but doubtful as to the propriety of accepting such bounty from one who was a stranger to him, Dominic allowed his sister to scold briskly over his rebellious behaviour and ingratitude before he counter-attacked.

"I'm not ungrateful. I just didn't want to go. Lord Valminster was in the right of it. On a journey like that Uncle Everard and I simply wouldn't have suited. I should have made him as miserable as he would have made me. He's a regular trump, isn't he? Lord Valminster. What's the nephew like? And do you think I ought to accept? And most of all, what sort of a May game d'you think you're playing? I scarcely knew you till you gave me the sign. You look quite hideous."

"Yes, don't I?" agreed his sister cordially. "I meant to. But it's too long a story to tell you now. Come down to the paddock with me and meet the others. Beatrice is about your age but the other three are younger. The nephew that his lordship meant is Benedict. He's twelve. I think you'll like him. I do. And I must admit it would be delightful to have you here for the holidays. We've planned all sorts of excursions. As for your being good for

Benedict, I don't know. I suppose so, just as I expect it was good for *you* to have two older brothers to see you kept the line. But only if you take to each other."

So far as could be judged on short acquaintance, this seemed highly probable. Horses supplied the vital link. After several minutes spent in discussing the style of Adam's pony— and in giving its rider one or two hints—Benedict invited the newcomer to come down to the stables with him and inspect his own two hacks. Graine left them to it, herself fully engaged in answering questions about her brother, the other members of her family, what horses and dogs they all kept, and was this the brother who had owned the grass snake? Wisely she made no mention of the invitation that his lordship had issued. Dominic had a streak of rigid honesty in his make-up. He might not want to go to Rome, but unless he felt that he could in some sort repay his host for hospitality so generously offered, neither would he come to Valminster. She awaited the return of the stable party with considerable curiosity and some anxiety. His lordship's solution of the problem seemed to her to be an ideal one. Dominic could always spend the holiday with their married sister, but Bridget was expecting to be confined in August and would be in no case to give much attention to the entertainment of an energetic schoolboy. Moreover her husband was a good deal older than she, and was stigmatized by his young brother-in-law as dull and pompous. She could not help hoping that Dominic and Benedict would take to each other.

She need not have been anxious. As the pair returned she heard Benedict's voice, pitched higher in his excitement, announce, "And you can ride Boxer. He's not really quite big enough for you, but I expect Uncle Ross will let you ride some of *his* horses as soon as he sees you're to be trusted. I shall tell Mrs Palmer to give you the room next to mine. I've got old Read on the other side, but he won't bother us much. I just wish your sister liked riding. We could have some splendid picnics."

Dominic looked incredulous. For the moment he had forgotten that he was pledged to secrecy about his sister's peculiar activities. "Not like riding? Rainey? You must be joking. Why she's an absolute—" There he remembered and broke off short. Fortunately his hearer's attention had been distracted by the use of the pet name.

"We thought she might be afraid of horses. Perhaps because of her lameness," said Benedict awkwardly. And then, eagerly, "*What* did you call her?"

"Rainey? We've always called her that, ever since she was about four years old."

They had now joined the group in the paddock which was happily engaged in feeding carrots to Adam's pony. Dominic looked up at his sister with a wicked glint worthy of Benedict himself.

"Yes, tell them," she said resignedly. She might have known that these two would get on together. There was a matching streak of devilment in both.

"She had such a tender heart," Dominic told the delighted children. "She couldn't bear the pigs to be killed or the chickens to have their necks wrung. If she herself fell down and cut her knees or bumped her nose, she would like as not grin and bear the pain bravely. But if her pet mouse died or the gardener drowned a litter of unwanted kittens, there were floods of tears. Truly floods. They just poured out—like rain. So because she was christened Graine, we called her Rainey. And of course it stuck."

For once it was not Benedict who made the obvious move. Young Bridget, emboldened by the glorious fact that her godmother was sister to these two interesting creatures, which seemed to give her some sort of claim to their attention, said timidly, "Couldn't *we* call you Rainey? It's so much more friendly than Miss Ashley. And you are a friend, aren't you? You told Uncle Ross so only yesterday when he was asking if we were well behaved."

Graine flung an arm round the slim shoulders and hugged the child.

"I would like it very much," she said, "if your uncle does not disapprove. Governesses are supposed to be dignified, you know, and he might not care for the idea of pet names for them."

A chorus of expostulation assured her that Uncle Ross was not so stuffy. "After all," said Benedict reasonably enough, "he lets us call him Uncle Ross, and it's not his name at all. Only he was Lord Rossingdon before he succeeded to the title, and all his friends called him Ross. He's got half a dozen names that I can't remember except that the first one's Mervyn. But it wouldn't seem a bit right to call him Uncle Mervyn. So you see."

Graine—now Rainey—did. It seemed that she was to enjoy a lively summer, full of temptations to which she must not succumb, steering a difficult course between the stiff, prim governess and Rainey, friend and confidante of the family. It was too soon to say whether her own brother would be a help or a hindrance in her delicate rôle.

Four

The holidays came, and Dominic with them.
His visit was an instant success. He fitted
into the Browning family as though he had
been born to it. But he was soon to find his
rôle beset by difficulties. It is not easy to be
the confidante of opposing interests, especially when both Bea and Benedict had taken
the precaution of pledging him to secrecy
where his sister might be concerned by their
schemes. The time came, regrettably soon,
when he felt that his new position of adult
responsibility demanded that he break this
pledge. It cost him a severe struggle. A fellow
did not lightly break his given word. But he

felt that Bea's affairs were moving out of his control, and he scented danger.

He came to his sister one afternoon, soon after schoolroom tea. Benedict and Adam had gone out to fish for the evening rise. Bridget had gone to take tea with one of her new friends.

"Where's Bea?" demanded Dominic bluntly.

Graine looked surprised. "She went out to finish her water colour sketch of the fountain," she replied.

"Well she's not there now," returned Dominic. "I came up through the rose gardens and she was nowhere in sight. I'm afraid the silly little idiot may have gone off on this ridiculous ploy of getting her fortune told."

Graine was roused to instant alarm, but there was no hurrying her brother. He must tell his story in his own fashion.

"It started when you went to the fair," he began. "Seems there was some gypsy woman that was telling fortunes and she wanted to have hers done, but Uncle Ross would have none of it. Which only made her all the more set on it, of course. That wouldn't have mattered a scrap, but the old dame's grandson had got himself a job in the stables. She—the grannie—took poorly after the fair, and they didn't move on with the rest of the tribe. The boy, Jake, seems to be quite a handy sort of lad. Even Jenkinson says that he shapes well,

58

though he doesn't expect him to stick to the
job for long. Seems that's the trouble with
gypsy blood. They're born wanderers. However, the difficulty at the moment is that he's
for ever hanging round Bea, when he gets the
chance. And she, the young minx, encourages
him because she hopes he'll take her to see
his grannie and she'll get her fortune told.
No harm in it, mind you. She just smiles at
him prettily when he brings her mare out,
and he moons after her. All a pack of silly
nonsense but it'll have to be stopped. It's not
fair to the lad, and Bea doesn't realise what
a peck of trouble she's stirring up. I promised
I wouldn't tell you, but if she's really gone off
to this wretched caravan, some one must go
and fetch her back."

"Indeed yes," agreed his sister. "But are
you quite sure that she has gone?"

"Soon find out," said Dominic.

"But don't betray her to anyone else," cau-
tioned his sister. "The less noise we make
about such an escapade—if she really *has*
gone—the better."

"I know that much, stupid," retorted Dominic with affectionate scorn. "Why else d'you
think I came to you?"

He strolled off down to the stables with the
negligent air of one who was merely filling
in time, assured himself that the gig was
missing and fell into casual talk with the

head groom, Jenkinson, asking if the new boy was still giving satisfaction. Jenkinson was non-committal.

"Got a good eye for a horse, I'll not deny. And give him something that he likes doing and he works with a will. He's gone off now, driving Miss Bea over to visit old Nancy that used to be her mother's nurse, and he's got the gig spruced up like it was the coronation coach." He chuckled. "Helps the work nicely, Mr Dominic, when a young fellow's mooning after one of the ladies of the house. Only the best is good enough for them. I well remember how I carried on myself in similar case."

He pulled himself up short, recalling that his auditor was rather young to be the recipient of such confidences. "But he's a fly-by-night—a light-weight—no bottom. No, that's not quite right," he ruminated thoughtfully. "He's got plenty of pluck." And then, suddenly inspired, "He's a here-and-thereian, that's what he is."

Dominic grinned, added one or two favourable comments on Jake's general smartness and cheerful air, and strolled away as casually as he had come. Once out of sight of the stable he quickened his pace considerably.

"Just as we feared," he burst in upon the anxious Graine. "They've gone off together in the gig. Supposedly visiting her Mama's

old nurse, who, I'll lay you odds, is already
in bed if not asleep. No. They've gone to visit
Jake's grannie. Luckily he happened to mention the fact that the caravan is standing in
Prince's Glen, just at the far end of the Royal
Ride. He was telling me that the gypsies have
claimed the right to camp there for over a
hundred years, and his lordship has never
disputed the privilege. It's no more than half
a mile, and if you want the business hushed
up, we'd better walk it."

They were both good walkers and anxiety
lent wings to their heels. In less than quarter
of an hour they were approaching Prince's
Glen. And there, sure enough, stood the Valminster gig, the sturdy brown cob tied to a
tree near a shabby gypsy caravan. An ancient
piebald horse was cropping the short turf. He
did not even raise his head at their approach.
An iron pot suspended over a small fire was
giving out savoury odours. There was no
other sign of habitation.

They advanced rather tentatively, Graine
trying to steady her hurried breathing. The
door of the caravan stood open, and as they
approached the sound of voices reached their
ears. One was young and feminine and
sounded fiercely angry, but since it spoke in
a strange language they were given no clue
as to the reason for that anger. Jake's voice,
deeper, slower, answering in the same lan-

guage sounded half apologetic. They heard him go on in English, "She says Grandma is too ill to be bothered with the likes of you, and that I was wrong to bring you. The sooner I take you home again, the better."

Bea's voice, a little timid, but with a note of determination in its soft cadences, said, "I don't wish to be a trouble to any one, but she doesn't *look* very ill. Perhaps I could come again-in a day or two, but it is very difficult to make excuses to slip away."

There came a crack of aged laughter. "It's in the right of it you are, milady, and not such a ninny as you look. I'm none so sick as Margarita here makes out. It suited her, you see, to stay behind and tend me, and her and Jake as good as tokened. You couldn't expect her to welcome a visit from the young lady that's got her chal fairly beglamoured."

Graine felt slightly sick. An unpleasant situation indeed. But there was no help for it. She climbed the two steps to the open door and knocked. There was immediate silence. She stepped inside. "May we come in?" she said pleasantly. "I must apologise for this intrusion, but we have come to take Miss Browning home, and it is already growing late. Are you ready, Beatrice?"

The gypsy girl had swung round with a belligerent air at the sound of the new voice, head flung back and arms akimbo. But evidently she understood English well enough for she relaxed visibly at these words. Jake looked shamefaced and Beatrice coloured to the roots of her hair. Only the old lady propped up in the narrow bed seemed unperturbed.

"That will be best," she commended calmly, and then turned to Beatrice.

"You don't need the likes of me to tell your fortune, child. You have gold and silver aplenty, and noble blood and a pretty face. Good friends, too." She glanced with regal approval at Graine and Dominic. "Those are your fortune. But one more word I have for you. Keep to your own kind and don't meddle with a world that's strange to you. That way danger lies. There. That is all the fortune you will have of me. Pay heed to it." She turned to Graine. "No need to be anxious, lady. No harm has come to the girl, nor will. By tomorrow we shall be gone from here."

Graine could only mutter slightly incoherent thanks and good wishes for the old woman's complete recovery. She had no money with her, and in any case she felt that any offer of reward would be an insult in the face of that calm dignity. She could only press the wrinkled hand and repeat her thanks.

The old woman's clasp on her fingers tightened, the intent dark eyes gazed earnestly into hers. "*You* are the one with the fine fortune, lady," she said slowly. "A long way off yet, but sure as tomorrow's dawn. Danger I see, and difficulty and sorrow, but great happiness to amend all." She almost flung Graine's hand away from her and said in quite a different voice, rough and harsh, "Be off with you now. We've much to do if we're to be on the road at first light."

They went thankfully. Dominic had a few shillings in his pocket which he finally persuaded Jake to accept, since by leaving in such a fashion he was forfeiting his wages. Then the boy untied the cob while Dominic helped the girls into the gig and took the reins. They did not talk until they had left the track and the caravan behind them. Then, as Dominic shook the cob into a gentle trot, Beatrice said penitently, "I'm sorry, Miss Ashley. I didn't think there was any harm in it. I didn't know about Margarita and that I was making trouble between her and Jake. I only wanted to hear my fortune. I was very thankful when you and Dominic came. They were so cross, and not even Jake would take my part. I was never so glad of anything in my life as when you knocked on that door."

She did indeed look pale and tired. Obviously the evening's events had shocked and frightened her. Graine thought she might well take the old gypsy woman's warning to heart, and could not bring herself to add a scolding of her own.

"The thing we must think about now is how to smuggle you back into the house without any one being the wiser," she said cheerfully. "The fewer people to know about this prank, the better. I am sure you will behave more sensibly in future."

Dominic could not foresee any particular difficulty about their return. He would see to the gig and the cob and engage himself to make all right with Jenkinson about Jake's departure. All that the girls had to do was to slip into the house unobtrusively. It was most likely that they had not even been missed.

It was unfortunate that Jake had not bestowed the same care on the state of the brown cob's shoes as he had devoted to the polishing of the gig. One of them had worked loose, and Dominic was obliged to get down and lead him to avoid the danger of a serious stumble. The delay was considerable, and to add to their discomfort it came on to rain. Graine decided that it would be quicker to take a short cut through the formal gardens instead of going all the way round by the stables, so leaving her brother to deal with the unfortunate cob, she and Beatrice hurried along the damp paths to the house and slipped in through the conservatory, thankful that Bosworth had not yet locked up for the night.

This relief was short-lived. The conservatory opened into the large drawing room, an apartment which, during the period of Graine's residence at Valminster had never been used. It was in use tonight. The Earl was showing his collection of miniatures to a lady and gentleman whom she had never seen before. It was impossible for the guilty pair to escape unseen. The Earl presented them casually to Mr and Mrs Barrington—his niece, Beatrice, and her governess, Miss Ashley—and all the time his eyes were roving thoughtfully over the two damp, dishevelled figures from untidy hair to muddy slippers.

"You are very wet," he said quietly. "Better put on some dry things. I would like a word with you later, Miss Ashley. I will come up to the schoolroom. Good night, Beatrice."

"He's going to ask where we've been," exclaimed Beatrice on a half sob as they went upstairs. Tears were not far away.

"I don't suppose so for a moment," lied Graine valiantly. "It's probably something quite different. Away to bed with you, and get Ellen to bring you a hot drink, or you'll be taking a chill. See, you're shivering."

Beatrice turned and hugged her impulsively. "If Benedict was here he'd say you were a regular trump. You won't let *me* say it, but you *are*, just the same."

Graine changed hurriedly into dry garments, smoothed her hair and repaired her 'complexion', which had not been improved by the rain. She settled down to await his lordship's arrival with considerable apprehension.

It was not unfounded. He attacked immediately.

"Nine o'clock is far too late for Beatrice to be out, Miss Ashley, unless the expedition has her Mama's approval, or, in the present circumstances, mine. Perhaps you will be so good as to tell me where she has been."

Graine hesitated. Then she said levelly, "She took a fancy to visit her mother's old nurse." That was at least partly true. It was the excuse that Beatrice had given for ordering the gig.

"Don't lie to me," he said sternly. "Old Nancy has been in her bed these two hours and more. You *must* think me a slow-top to swallow such an unlikely tale."

He surveyed her in silence for what seemed an age, the grey eyes raking her face with merciless directness. She faced his inquisitorial stare bravely enough, but she could not prevent her colour from rising. Fortunately the full effect was masked by her grease paint. She also put up a nervous hand to brush back a curl of damp hair that had escaped its restraining pin. His face softened a little. He said calmly, "Beatrice is in some scrape and you are trying to cover up for her. Pray don't. I appreciate your loyalty and am happy to know that you have taken your charges in affection, but if she *is* in a scrape it would be much more sensible to let me deal with it. I promise not to scold her beyond what is reasonable."

"Beatrice *was* in a scrape, and all of her own making," interjected a new voice. Graine and his lordship swung round to face the little figure in the doorway. Very small and young she looked, a wrapper over her nightdress, her hair in two thick plaits, but very determined, too. She stood there for a moment surveying them, then ran across the intervening space to cast herself into her uncle's arms.

He hugged her reassuringly close before drawing her towards the hearth where a cheerful fire still glowed and settling her in one of the schoolroom's shabby but comfortable chairs. "Now tell me all about it," he bade her.

"I was afraid you were going to blame Miss Ashley," she explained, quite unconsciously earning herself a place in her uncle's respect, "and it was nothing to do with her."

The whole story tumbled out. Having been assured that her uncle would not scold her 'above what was reasonable', she told a straightforward tale. She had wanted to have her fortune told, and the employment of Jake in the stables had seemed to offer an opportunity of arranging this. That was all she had thought about.

It was perhaps natural that the recital should end in a burst of tears as she thought of the trouble she had made, not only between Jake and Margarita but also in part for the old grandmother and for Miss Ashley, too. All of them had been caught up in her idle whim, for as such she now saw it. His lordship patted, consoled and reasoned with her. Miss Ashley could not but admire his handling of the situation, and thought what an excellent parent he would make.

When Beatrice had finally been despatched to bed, with a promise that Graine would come in later to see that she was comfortably settled, his lordship did not at once take his departure.

"I confess that I was very doubtful about your method of handling this particular problem," he told Graine soberly. "But I will freely admit that the outcome was admirable. Beatrice made a full confession of her own accord, rather than see you suffer for her fault. One may hope, too, that she will have gained confidence in both of us. Nevertheless, Miss Ashley, I hope that in future you will turn to me, rather than to your brother, when you need masculine support in your duties."

"Well as to that, sir, it was thanks to Dominic that the whole business was brought to light, and by that time it was too late to consult any one else if we were to get Beatrice home before the darkening. But I wish you will comfort Dominic, if you would be so good. It seems that he came by his knowledge of the projected expedition under promise of respecting the confidence reposed in him. I have assured him that his action in coming to me was both sensible and adult, but he only says that females do not properly understand such matters, and he is much exercised in his mind as to how Benedict will regard his breach of faith. I would be very grateful if you would add your assurances to mine."

"It is a nice point," admitted his lordship. "I am deeply grateful for Dominic's sensible action, yet I fully enter into his feelings about keeping a promise of secrecy. I will certainly do my possible to set his mind at rest. Meanwhile, Miss Ashley, my sincere thanks for your very valuable assistance tonight."

Five

Graine never knew what passed between her brother and his lordship, but the latter seemed to have succeeded to admiration in the task that she had given him. Beatrice and Dominic were on the best of terms, and Benedict's admiration for the older boy did not falter.

Since Benedict was to go to school after the holiday, Mr Read had taken his departure. This to Dominic's great content, since he felt that the Earl trusted him to exercise a fraternal supervision over Benedict, and that his position was not just a sinecure. To Benedict's great satisfaction, too, until he realised that his new keeper maintained a much stricter watch on all his comings and goings than ever Mr Read had done, and that it was not near so easy to pull the wool over his eyes. Fortunately they were so much in sympathy that it was generally easy for Dominic to dissuade the younger boy from some of his more hazardous enterprises and to suggest alternatives that were much to his taste. The Earl, strolling out in the evening coolness to cast an amused eye on a game of cricket that was in progress on Gatehouse Green, did not even utter a mild protest about the cutting up of the smooth turf, though the head gardener had earnestly assured him that it would take years to restore it to its pristine perfection. Henry, the young footman, and two of the grooms had been pressed into service to give the opposing teams some substance, and Henry had proved to be a demon bowler of erratic length who could make the ball bounce in a most unpredictable fashion. Benedict was standing up to him manfully, determined not to flinch under the watchful eye of his new mentor.

The Earl strolled across to the far side of the Green where Miss Ashley had been posted in the field. She had very little to do, since most of Henry's deliveries were unplayable, so was able to lend a gratified ear to his praise of her brother.

"Nothing could have answered better," he told her. "Read was by far too stuffy for a lively youngster, though a hard worker and eminently worthy. But Benedict will learn more from your brother in a sennight. The things that are not to be found in lesson books. I take credit to myself for having assessed Dominic's quality so swiftly. And I think I owe you an apology for having *under* estimated yours."

She turned her head swiftly to look at him. It was the first time that he had spoken to her naturally as to an equal, and she scarcely knew how to answer.

She was spared the trouble. At that moment came a concerted yell from the entire fielding side. Benedict had succeeded in smiting one of Henry's deliveries. He had hit it hard and true, but owing to the peculiarity of its bounce it had gone soaring up into the blue and was descending in the vicinity of the inattentive Miss Ashley.

The Earl could not be expected to resist. Two long strides to his right and an arm reached up and plucked the ball from the air, tossing it from palm to palm to exaggerate the insult. There was a loud "Huzzah!" from Dominic, captain of the fielding side, and the game broke up in a cheerful wrangle as to whether a man was really out when he was caught by an unauthorised person (Benedict's argument) interrupted by Henry's expressions of satisfaction at having someone caught off his bowling by the Earl himself and Benedict's own pride in that one capital hit that, but for Uncle Ross's interference, would certainly have gone for four.

It was unfortunate that a week of very wet weather should interfere with their pleasant existence. There could be no prospect of rides or picnic excursions while the rain was teeming down, and even Graine's ingenuity was taxed by the effort of devising entertainment for her charges. When all the time-honoured expedients had been tried, she coaxed them into devising a play, which, she promised, if it was good enough, they could perform for the visiting notabilities and the village folk at a forthcoming Public Day.

But interest was spasmodic. Beatrice was enthusiastic, Dominic dutiful. The younger children copied their elders and Benedict was the genie out of the bottle. If he was in the right mood he could bring the whole thing to life. If he was not he could disrupt it entirely. Graine could only be thankful when the rain eased up and it was possible to get the children out of doors again.

It was a soaked and dripping world after a night of steady rain, and the weather was still unsettled. Graine felt that it would be too risky to go far afield, but the children pleaded for a picnic.

"Couldn't we go to the glen?" suggested

Benedict. "The stones by the brookside soon dry and the waterfalls will be very pretty after the rain."

It was quite a sensible suggestion. The glen was a favourite place with the whole family. A small stream ran through it and descended in several modest falls from the moorland heights that had given it birth to the gentle levels of the water garden. The skill of the landscape gardener had been employed to make the most of this promising material. Paths had been laid to follow the course of the stream, steps had been skilfully contrived to make the changing levels easy of access, and the whole had been framed in a 'wild' garden where flowering shrubs brought from foreign lands had been planted to add colour to nature's own provision. The glen was lovely at any season, even in severe winters when the stream froze and turned the little waterfalls into fantastic castles and fairy palaces of ice. And it was true that the stones that bordered the stream would dry out more quickly than other possible picnic spots.

"Very well," agreed Graine. "A picnic lunch. Do you go and tell Mrs Palmer, Beatrice."

As soon as the girl had gone she turned swiftly to Benedict. "And if you go by the top road I could take the lower path and meet you at the Cavern Fall with picnic baskets.

That would give me half the morning to finish the lining of Bea's work-box."

The box in question was designed as a gift for Beatrice, whose birthday fell in a few days' time. Benedict had made it, working industriously and for once obedient to advice, keeping it a close secret in the carpenter's shop, and Graine had undertaken to line it. But the lining must be quilted, the edges ruched and scalloped, and it was difficult to find time to work on it when Beatrice was not present. Graine was a little uneasy at the thought of sending the children off on their own, bursting with energy and high spirits as they were after the long confinement to the house. But Dominic and Beatrice were sensible enough and they would not be going outside the bounds of the Valminster estates. It was difficult to see what mischief they could fall into in one short morning walk. She could put in an hour's work on the box lining and by taking the short cut along the lower road to the glen could keep her rendezvous with the rest of the party before their appetites became too sharp-set.

She was unaware that at that very moment Dominic was hastily changing into riding breeches, his lordship having requested the pleasure of his company on a ride to one of the outlying farms.

"I want to see how you can handle Crusader," he had said bluntly. "He might be a little too strong for you, but he hasn't a scrap of vice. See how he goes for you. He could do with regular exercise—more than he gets. I mean to hunt him next season."

Dominic completed his hasty toilet, glanced in the mirror to make sure that his stock was setting properly, and ran down to the hall where he found Graine putting letters in the postbag. His face was alight with excitement as he told her of milord's suggestion. She could not bear to see him dashed down, so good and helpful as he had been.

"Oh dear!" she sighed. "And I did want to finish Bea's work-box. Never mind. I will go with the children this morning, and perhaps you can think of some ploy to keep Bea out of the way at another time."

"He will do no such thing," announced a quiet voice behind her. His lordship had come into the hall from the library and had overheard the latter part of the conversation. "You have had no time to yourself ever since you came. We have all been very selfish, but I am to blame for the oversight. Except that you yourself are partly to blame, because you seem so much one of the family that one tends to impose on your good nature. Now, what is the problem?"

Graine, her blushes at the delightful compliment fortunately masked by grease paint, explained that she had been relying on Dominic to keep superabundant high spirits within bounds. "They pay more heed to him than they do to Bea," she ended apologetically. "Probably because he is *not* their brother."

"For which, no doubt, he renders daily thanks," nodded his lordship. "Well the matter is quite simple. The picnic will proceed as arranged, and you will stay at home and devote your free morning to the embellishment of Beatrice's birthday gift. The children can come to no harm if they do as you have planned. And once Beatrice's birthday is safely past, you must have a *really* free day. Do something of your own choosing, not necessarily designed for the enjoyment and betterment of your charges."

She gave a little chuckle for that. Dominic was all a-grin, so pleased he was that the morning's ride need not be abandoned. And his lordship was even better than his word. He himself charged Bea and Benedict as to their behaviour on the excursion. They were to do precisely as Miss Ashley—he had not yet fallen into the habit of addressing her as Rainey, as the others did, though once or twice it had risen unbidden to his lips—had arranged, and they were not to stray away from the agreed meeting point until she arrived.

As usual, Benedict had the last word. "Not

likely, sir," he assured his uncle. "*She* will have the food."

The party dispersed about their various activities, Graine assuring herself that all the younger children were wearing sturdy shoes that would stand up to walking on wet rock before waving them away on their expedition and retiring to her own room and her needle.

With nothing to distract her she made good progress, and was ready to set out a little before noon, which was just as well since the picnic baskets were quite heavy and slowed her speed considerably. Almost she wished that she had requested the services of Henry to carry them for her, and was still smiling at the thought that they would be a good deal lighter on the return journey when she reached the bank of the stream which she must follow for the last part of her walk. She gave a gasp of amazement. The gentle little brook that normally shrank in places to the merest trickle had been transformed into a rushing, turbulent flood of brown, foam-flecked water.

Her heart-beats quickened with apprehension. She ought to have realised that the persistent rain of the previous week, crowned by yesterday's downpour, must naturally swell the stream. This was no safe place to send children to play. The pretty little brook was a potential killer. She set down the baskets

and began to run towards the Cavern Fall,
thankful for the well-laid paths that permitted her to make good speed.

Her fears were well founded. She had run
no more than a hundred yards or so when she
recognised a small figure racing towards her.
Benedict. And only disaster in one form or
another could have caused him to break his
word to his uncle and leave the appointed
rendezvous.

She ran on till she was breathless and had
a stitch in her side, and sank gasping on to
a boulder that edged the path as Benedict
came up to her. His face was crimson with
his exertions and he was sobbing for breath,
his whole appearance that of shock and desperation.

"It's Adam and Bridget," he panted out as
soon as he had breath enough. "They were in
the cave behind the fall when the flood came
down. It came so suddenly. They can't get
back till the water goes down, and they're
frightened. They were both crying. I left Beatrice to watch over them and came for help."

"And you did very right," she told him in
as calm a voice as she could muster, for she
herself was badly frightened but must make
what effort she could to calm the shaken boy.

As long as the children stayed where they
were, they were fairly safe. The cave behind
the Cavern Fall wasn't really a cave at all.

Its peculiarity was that over the centuries
the falling water had hollowed out the per-
pendicular face of the rock so that now, when
there was a moderate fall of water, it was
possible to walk along a narrow ledge between the rock face and the falling water,
perfectly safe and dry, gazing out through the
veil of water at the lower reaches of the
stream. Graine herself had done it several
times, and the children loved it, though
Graine had once or twice suspected that
young Bridget had to nerve herself to take
the narrow path. But to be trapped on that
ledge while the present peat-brown torrent
hurtled over one was a very different matter.
It would be terrifying. The noise would be
stunning, the sliding speed of the flood almost
hypnotic. Graine could only feel deeply anxious. She said, "If you have got your wind,
run on up to the house. Get some of the
grooms—young, strong ones—to bring the
longest ladders they can find to the Cavern
Fall. And ropes. It might be possible to push
a ladder along the ledge behind the water,
and a man, securely held by ropes from the
bank, could make his way along it to reach
the children. It would give them comfort and
confidence, even if they must wait some hours
for actual rescue."

Benedict was off again almost before she

had finished speaking, and she herself wasted no time in setting off upstream.

The sight that met her eyes at the Cavern Fall was a shocking one by any standards, quite appalling in the eyes of a governess who could only feel that she had failed in her duty. Beatrice was crouched alone on the verge of the stream. She had been trying to call messages of encouragement to her brother and sister, but it was impossible to tell if they could hear her above the thunder of the flood. Certainly *she* could not hear their replies if they made any. And she no sooner set eyes on Graine than she burst into tears and had to be rather firmly quieted.

It was impossible to see the trapped children through the volume of water that was pouring over the fall, but a tearful Beatrice, still gulping back sobs, showed her how one could just pick out the two figures huddled together against the wet rock face by peering round the edge of it. There was no indication that they had noticed Graine's arrival. They did not wave or call out—or if they did their childish voices were lost in the howling tumult.

Anxiously Graine calculated that it would take at least another half hour for help to arrive. The children must already be soaked to the skin, for the ledge on which they were sitting was under water. If they grew numbed

with cold it would be even more difficult for
them to cling to their precarious perch. And
the pool into which the stream emptied itself
was deep enough to drown a child in normal
conditions. With the present flood beating
down on its surface, neither of them would
stand a chance. She looked at the path that
led to the ledge and made up her mind. There
was only one really dangerous place, where
a break in the lip at the edge of the fall permitted a quantity of water to slide down the
face of the rock. It was no more than a foot
wide, but for the time that it took to cross it
the person who ventured to challenge the
power of the flood would be subjected to its
full fury. The only comfort she could see was
a very solid looking lump of rock some three
feet high on the outer edge of the path. It did
not quite match the break at the top of the
fall, but it should be possible to cling to it. At
least it might prevent a would-be rescuer
from being swept into the abyss.

"I'm going across to them," she told Beatrice. "At least I can tell them that help is on
the way, and try to support their spirits."

Beatrice stared at her, wide-eyed, but could
not reject any proposal that might bring a
morsel of comfort to the children.

"And you are to stay here," went on Graine,
almost fiercely. "Whatever happens you are

to stay here until Benedict brings help. You understand?"

Beatrice nodded mutely. She understood only too well. In the next few minutes she might well see Miss Ashley swept to her death, without being able to lift a finger to help.

Graine wasted no more time. The path led directly to the ledge of rock where the children were trapped. Water was swirling over it, but it was no more than an inch deep. She took no unnecessary risks. On the wet rock a slip or a stumble was all too probable. It was no time to be considering one's dignity. She dropped to all fours and crawled steadily to the beginning of the ledge. Here the surface water was a little deeper and spray from the falling flood was continually dashed into her face, half blinding her and filling her nostrils, but she struggled on until she reached the rock that she had noted from the bank. Here she paused for a moment, clinging to the rock with one hand while she dashed the water from her face with the other and filled her aching lungs. The next bit of her passage was the dangerous part. No use delaying. She was frightened enough already. She gripped the edge of her friendly rock and set off.

For a moment, as the weight of the falling water struck her, she thought that she had been swept from her refuge into the stream itself. Had it not been for the partial shelter she had found, she must have perished in the churning brown water of the pool. Thanks to her grasp on the rock, somehow she inched her way forward, deafened, battered, intent only on reaching the two castaways whom she could now see clearly. Then she was through, and crawling along the rock towards them.

They were still very precariously placed. Even where the ledge was widest, no more than three or four feet separated them from tumbling water. Graine settled herself between the children, an arm round each, hugging them close to her, trying to assure them that help was on the way. They seemed to be half dazed and she could not tell if they had understood, or even if they had heard her, but they clutched her fiercely as though she was their one hope and she held them tight and crooned a little wordless song that none of them could hear amid the clamour of the water, but which somehow comforted Graine. It was as though she was defying the flood to do its worst, saying that she had the children safe and would keep them so.

Nevertheless it seemed a very long time before the rescue party arrived. Graine watched the racing water. Was she imagining it, or was the level already falling slightly? Presently she was sure of it. There was less water on the ledge itself, though there was still a substantial stream coming down from the fault. By the time that Benedict, with half a dozen grooms and two long ladders came panting up the last flight of steps that led to the fall, the ledge on which the three prisoners were sitting was practically clear of standing water.

From that point the work of rescue went swiftly if not without difficulty. With the ladder to provide a reasonable hold, the first groom managed to reach the ledge much as Graine had done. The ledge was now distinctly overpopulated and its occupants had to move with extreme care, but with Graine's assistance Adam was successfully roped to the groom's back and carried along the ladder bridge to safety. A second man performed a like service for Bridget. Graine felt very much like saying that she would wait until the flood subsided. Once—and without a ladder—was enough. But such an admission was unworthy of her Ashley blood. Nor would she consent to being carried, though, as the groom pointed out, she was not so much heavier than Miss Bridget. Instead she agreed to having a rope tied about her in case of mishap and scrambled across the ladder on hands and knees, arriving just in time to be assisted to dry land by no less a person than the Earl himself, who, with Dominic, had just arrived on the scene.

Soaked, battered, dishevelled, she stared up at him dumbly, vainly seeking words to express her contrition. There were no such words in her vocabulary. Then the groom who was hauling the ladder ashore slipped on the wet rock just as he had the ladder poised almost vertically. It jerked from his grasp and descended, it seemed with deliberate intent, to strike her a glancing blow on the side of her head. She subsided—perhaps thankfully—into unconsciousness.

Six

She woke in her own comfortable bed in the
pleasant room that was beginning to feel like
home. Her head ached badly, but her memory
of the events of the morning was perfectly
clear. Too clear, she thought with a slight
shudder, recalling the moment when she had
thought herself swept away by the stream.
She could even remember the ladder tilting
towards her and her attempt to avoid it. Running tenderly explorative fingers over her
head she came to the conclusions that the
attempt had not been successful. But at least
the children were safe, and compared with
that nothing else mattered very much.

Except the danger of dismissal. As this

unpleasant thought suddenly occurred to her she jerked up her head sharply, causing it to throb more painfully than ever. There could be no evading the unpleasant truth. If she had gone with the children this morning they would never have been in danger. She would have noticed the increased volume of the stream and would certainly have forbidden them to risk going into the cave. It was true that his lordship had given her permission to take a morning's holiday, but a truly conscientious governess would not have availed herself of that permission. The more she thought about it the more likely it seemed that she stood in grave danger of losing a post that suited her better than any she had ever held, and the thought that Dominic too, would be involved in her downfall was the last straw. She turned her aching head into the pillow and gave way to tears.

A cautious tap on her door, followed by the gentle lifting of the latch, put an end to this orgy of self pity. She hurriedly mopped her face and struggled up into a sitting position to confront her visitor, despite the pain in her head. It was Beatrice, carrying a small tray, which she set down on the table that stood beside the bed.

With a tact beyond her years the girl ignored the traces of tears and the occasional sob that still escaped the sufferer.

"Is your head *very* painful?" she enquired solicitously. "You have a great big lump on it where the ladder hit you, but Doctor Tempest said that there was no serious damage, and that you could get up as soon as you felt like it. And luckily your hair covers the bruise. Mrs Palmer has made you a cup of her herb tea, which she says will make you feel much more the thing, and Uncle Ross says that I am not to tease you to come down for dinner if you don't feel able for it, though he is just as impatient as the rest of us, wanting to thank you for what you did for Adam and Bridget."

Such an attitude did not seem to pose a threat of summary dismissal. Graine took heart, and sipped Mrs Palmer's offering cautiously. It was quite pleasant to the palate. She thought she could detect mint and sweet balm. At least it was hot, and soothing to a tear-swollen throat. Beatrice chatted on casually, bringing her up to date on the state of the family. Bridget and Adam had been put to bed. Doctor Tempest did not think they were much the worse for their ordeal, but wished to guard against the possibility of a serious chill. They had both slept long and soundly throughout the afternoon, and were now in tearing spirits, very full of themselves and their adventure, and clamouring to get up.

"Any one would think that *they* had shown true heroism," commented Beatrice, but her tone was indulgent.

"Well they *were* very plucky," suggested Graine. "They did well to hold out until help reached them. It was quite terrifying, I promise you."

"Bridget said she didn't think she could have lasted much longer if *you* hadn't got to them when you did," said Beatrice quietly. "Oh, darling Rainey, how can we ever thank you enough? Uncle Ross says *you* were the heroine of the occasion and that we owe you a debt that we can never repay. Just imagine if we had had to write and tell Mama—" and her own voice was suspended by emotion.

Whether it was the effect of Mrs Palmer's brew or of the heartening nature of these exchanges, Graine was beginning to feel very much better. This was fortunate, since there was another shock in store for her. When she announced her intention of dressing and coming downstairs, and rather gingerly tried the effect of standing up, Beatrice, offering to help her dress, said shyly, "Do you have to put that horrid stuff on your face, Rainey? Dr Tempest made us wash it all off. And the—the—mole on the side of your nose washed off, too, though I think that was the soaking it got at the Cavern Fall," she concluded hastily. She hesitated a moment, then burst out eagerly, "I'm sorry, Rainey. It was so strange that we asked Dominic. He admitted that it was a disguise, but he said that it was *your* secret. I don't mean to pry. Indeed I'd help you, any way I could, especially after what you've done for us. But you look so sweet without it. We couldn't help noticing the pads sewn into the shoulders of your shift, either. You're not really lame, are you? Benedict said you weren't. He'd noticed that already. All part of the disguise I suppose. Forgive me if I sound quizzy. I don't mean to. Only surely you can trust us now, even if you couldn't before. If there is some danger threatening you, can't we help?"

It was a moment for truth. Beatrice had opened her heart. Graine could do no less.

"There was a danger," she said slowly. "But because I was alone, I exaggerated it out of all proportions. Now, living here, in the heart of the family, I feel much safer. And I confess I will be truly thankful to be done with masquerading. It is amusing at first but soon grows wearisome and is very uncomfortable. It is not just the disguise, you see. That is simple. It is altering all your habits to match the disguise. If you only knew how I have longed to ride out with you all and have been compelled to stay stuffily at home. Not to mention sailing and swimming—because of the disguise, you understand. See what happened the first time I got a thorough soaking! Believe me, I shall be more than thankful to be done with it."

"So shall we," chuckled Beatrice contentedly. "Everything will be much more fun when you can share it with us."

She insisted on unpicking the padding that had simulated the deformed shoulder, and chose Graine's prettiest dress, though to be sure that was not saying a great deal, all of them having been chosen with an eye to sobriety. "And I'm sure your head will feel much more comfortable without that tight cap," she concluded. "Let me dress your hair. I will be very gentle and careful. Mama sometimes lets me do hers."

It was very pleasant to be fussed and babied in this affectionate way, but it was still something of an ordeal to face the assembled family at the dinner table. She could not help blushing a little as the little chorus of welcome greeted her changed appearance. His lordship said only, "Ah! I see," in a reflective sort of voice. But Dominic and Benedict had no such inhibitions, the one announcing thankfully that he was glad he need no longer blush for a sister who was a positive antidote, the other much more interested in the methods with which the effect had been achieved, and asking hopefully if he might experiment with Rainey's grease paints one day.

Graine's attempts to express her contrition
for her share in the morning's events were
courteously but very firmly silenced by his
lordship.

"If any one must take sole responsibility,
then I must," he said quietly. "And if any one
should have foreseen possible danger, I should.
I have lived here all my life and know how
swiftly the streams can flood after persistent
rain. I cannot acquit myself of heedlessness.
Nor can I express my gratitude for the cour-
age that you displayed. If you had not reached
the children when you did, help might well
have come too late. Benedict tells me, too,
that it was you who sent for ladders and
ropes. Competent as well as courageous. Once
before I said to you that I thought I had
underestimated your quality. I little knew
how much. But I will not embarrass you with
further praise. I think we would all be the
better for a new topic of conversation. Are
you going to take Crusader in hand for me,
Dominic, and get him into condition for the
hunting season?"

The talk thereafter centred on horses, the
Earl regretting that at present he had no an-
imal in his stables suitable for Graine to ride.
"There is Beatrice's Yorkshire Rose, but I
know you well enough to realise that you
would not dream of depriving Bea of her precious mare. Besides, you will wish to ride to-

gether. I take it, by the way, that you *do* ride, now that you are done with masquerading?"

There was a snort of laughter from Dominic. "Ride? Rainey? Just wait till you see her, sir. She could handle Crusader better than I can. Yes, I know he's too strong for her. It makes no difference. And I'm not just partial because she's my sister. It's a knack she has—like some people can sing and others paint. Rainey can whisper horses."

"She can *what*?" demanded the Earl, much intrigued by this new facet in the personality of the mouse-like governess.

"That's what my father's old stud groom used to call it," explained the boy. "Whispering. She doesn't actually talk to them or pet them more than other people do. It's a kind of a crooning. The horses seem to understand it, and they go for her when they would fight another rider. I've never seen the horse yet that she couldn't handle, though I'll admit that she rode some of them astride, which wouldn't do here, of course. But you've no need to fret over suitable mounts for a lady. Plenty of beasts in the stable that will carry a side saddle, so long as the rider's experienced."

"Now it is your turn to embarrass your sister," pointed out his lordship, smiling at the crimson-faced Graine. "And since you seem to have finished your dinner I am going to ask the three of you to leave her with me for a few moments so that she can recover her countenance. Miss Ashley, will you take a glass of wine with me?"

The youngsters took their dismissal in good part. Naturally Uncle Ross wanted to thank Rainey properly for what she had done, and equally naturally it would be embarrassing to be thanked in public. Graine declined the glass of wine, suggesting that, on top of a bump on the head, it might be a little too much for the sedate demeanour demanded of a governess.

"Which is precisely the point that I wish to discuss with you, Miss Ashley," rejoined his lordship. "Standing so deep in your debt as I do, I feel that I may speak more freely on this head than would otherwise be permissible. This disguise that you adopted. I do not wish to pry into your affairs, and I can understand that your present appearance, delightful as it is, might be a positive disadvantage to a young female pursuing the career of a governess. The sober gowns and the caps I could accept. But your disfiguring disguise went further than that. You seem to me to be a woman of good sense, not given to distempered freaks. Something of considerable import must have driven you to go to such lengths. If you are in any difficulty— even danger—that persuaded you so to disguise yourself, I am entirely at your command. You cannot doubt my willingness to serve you. Is there any way in which I can do so?"

For the third time that evening Graine was sunk in embarrassment. He was so simple, so sincere, that her masquerading seemed theatrical and paltry.

She said painfully, "You do me too much honour, milord. At the same time, you have gone to the nub of the matter. I do not wish to sound unduly conceited, but my normal appearance is more than disadvantageous to a governess. It is a disaster. I have been obliged to resign the last two posts that I have held—both of them otherwise extremely suitable—because of—of—"

"Undesirable masculine attentions," supplied his lordship smoothly.

She nodded, half thankful, half resentful to find him so swift of perception.

"So when you found yourself appointed to a household where there was no mistress to protect you, you took your own measures to guard your virtue. Very understandable, if a trifle excessive. In that case there is no more to be said, except to assure you that in this household you stand in no such danger and may safely revert to your normal habits."

After his professions of service that was a little too much for Graine's Irish temper. The events of the day had already strained her self control to the limit. It snapped.

"So far as you are concerned, milord, I am well aware," she curtsied. "And one cannot imagine Mr Read indulging a passion for anything more animated than a lexicon. But in my last situation it was not the gentlemen of the household who posed the problem but the male guests, so your kind assurances are of little worth. However, I thank you for them, and since you do not entertain extensively I shall hope to pursue my untroubled existence at least until your sister's plans are more settled."

At this point she recollected their respective positions and subsided into a welter of guilt and apology, pressing her hands to flushed cheeks and biting her soft lips together as though she was striving too late to repress her rash speech.

His lordship made no direct reply. "I really think you should take a small glass of wine, Miss Ashley," he told her kindly. "I feel that the strain of the day has taken its toll. I did not think to hear you speak so intemperately. Though I must confess that the thought of Mr Read and a lexicon is apt—very apt. As for house guests—you may count yourself safe until the shooting season begins."

He broke off abruptly, realising what he had said, his sober face relaxing into laughter. "An unfortunate choice of phrase. But you will take my meaning and understand that I intended no disparagement of the skill of my guests. And shall I sink myself beyond reproach if I acknowledge a certain degree of respect for the good taste, if not the behaviour, of your previous admirers?"

Seven

The change in Miss Ashley's appearance and demeanour was not even a nine days' wonder. Before the week was out it no longer provided cause for comment. Possibly the senior members of the staff had their own ideas as to the unprepossessing appearance that she had presented on her arrival. Possibly they approved. In any case, no one was prepared to voice either speculation, or criticism of the girl who had acted so promptly and bravely when the children of the house were in danger. The grooms who had been on the scene at the Cavern Fall had been enthusiastic in their praise of Miss Ashley's conduct. When her uncanny ability with horses was discovered, her position in their esteem rose even higher. Bosworth had liked her from the start. Mrs Palmer was prepared to respect one who could control her favourite, Benedict, without unduly repressing his high spirits, and unbent still further when the young lady showed a proper appreciation of the effects of her herb tea. Bridget and Adam had gaped a little at their first sight of the transformed Miss Ashley, but her standing in their affection had been secured once and for all on that beastly ledge. When they further discovered that she was now willing to ride with them and to join in all their outdoor ploys, no longer fearing that an accidental drenching might unmask her, they were well-pleased but not greatly surprised. The vagaries of grown-ups were incalculable any way. If Miss Ashley had chosen to behave so, no doubt she had had a good reason.

The only dissenting voice in this general chorus of approval—and it held its peace—was his lordship's. None of them held Miss Ashley in higher esteem, but none of them was so much affected by her new and bewitching appearance. True, she still affected the sober style of dress that she considered appropriate to her position, though she had easily been persuaded to discard her caps, compromising by dressing her hair in the plainest possible style. But hair that curls naturally does not readily submit to such strict discipline, and the active life that Miss Ashley now led gave it every opportunity of escaping from the smooth bands into which she had pinned it. There were usually errant curls or tendrils of the silky dark stuff waving about temples and nape.

The most striking change, however, was in her complexion. Her skin had that delicate transparency so often characteristic of Irish beauties. One longed to touch it to see if it really had that rose-petal smoothness that it suggested. Allied to those eyes that his lordship had acknowledged to be magnificent even at their first meeting, eyes of a smokey blue-grey, fringed by long dark lashes, the effect was devastating. His lordship who had begun to like Miss Ashley quite well towards the end of what he now thought of as her 'mouse masquerade', found that his sensations were no longer those of mild liking. It was not only her physical appearance that had changed. Now that she allowed her personality free play she was a vital, alluring creature, generous and warm-hearted. Her wit was more than adequate to the task of holding her own in some lively exchanges with her charges, and she had a happy knack of bringing out the best in them. His lordship, finding himself thinking what a delightful mother she would make, decided that he was growing maudlin and made a determined attempt to turn his thoughts to other matters. A slight difficulty had arisen over the freehold of a farm that he planned to purchase. He would write to his attorney to make sure that the title was perfectly clear before completing the transaction. He pulled the standish towards him and picked up his pen. Five minutes later, the paper still virgin beneath his hand, he was gloomily wondering if a ten year difference in age was an insuperable bar to matrimony. Graine was twenty seven, he knew. She had made no secret of it when she and Bea had been discussing the vexed question of wearing a cap.

Worst of all, of course, was the fact that he could make no attempt to fix his interest with her. Having rashly pledged his word that she need not fear masculine importunities while she resided under his roof, his hands were tied. He comforted himself with the thought that friendship must form a sound basis for a more intimate association, kept a strict guard on face and voice, and surrounded Miss Ashley with an unobtrusive care for her comfort that did far more for his cause than flamboyant compliments. Graine was not a romantically minded eighteen year old to be impressed by outward trappings, but close association with his lordship could not fail to teach her his good qualities. She found him just and kindly to his dependents, generous and affectionate to his family and friends, while his easy-going elder brother attitude to Dominic earned her passionate gratitude. Yet he was not such a paragon of all the virtues as to become boring or to make one feel hopelessly inferior. He could show anger and intolerance when his notions of proper behaviour were offended, or he could keep his family in tucks of laughter by his description of some small event that had tickled his sense of humour, or by tales of various escapades of his own youth. He seemed to spend a good deal of time with the children. Graine, who was accustomed to households where the parents handed over the entire care of their offspring to nurses, governesses and tutors, and sometimes permitted several days to elapse without so much as setting eyes on them, found this admirable, never dreaming that for once she was crediting his lordship with a virtue which he did not possess. The gentleman himself wondered if ever before a man had embarked on his courtship under the surveillance of a brace of nieces and nephews and his quarry's younger brother, but was far too wise to make any attempt to isolate Graine from her charges even when he might reasonably have done so. He did, however, spend a good deal of time in calculating how long it might be before his sister returned to

England. There had been some mention of Christmas, and that was four months away. Once Dominic and Benedict went off to school it would be more difficult to find excuses for joining in the activities of the schoolroom party. Besides, he was growing impatient. He was fairly confident that he had won Graine's liking. She treated him with frank confidence, turning to him in the most natural way for advice and support. But he wanted a good deal more than that, and not until she was established in his sister's house would he be free to woo her openly.

It was therefore with an unusual degree of interest that he opened a letter from Lady Elizabeth which had been brought by special courier.

It contained disturbing news. Sir John had met with an accident. His wife did not say how—the letter was written in haste and was rather disjointed—but he had broken a leg and several ribs and was likely to be laid up for some time. As Ross would know, he was the worst of patients, refusing to follow the physician's advice and determined on doing a number of imprudent things, one of which, since he declared he was, "Utterly useless in Copenhagen, laid by the heels as I am," was to return to England. He was really in no case to travel, but his wife could neither convince him of the folly of such a proceeding nor feel herself capable of taking charge of such a difficult journey if she let him have his way. She had won a brief respite by telling him that she was writing to her brother with a plea for help. Would Ross come over to Copenhagen, either to support her persuasions or, if Sir John remained adamant, to organise the return to England.

Ross considered carefully. The courier was able to tell him that Sir John had received his injuries in a carriage accident, and that he was going along pretty fairly, all things considered, but that her ladyship was in a rare taking, since Sir John was vowing that he had no faith in what he described as "Foreign sawbones", and meant to return to a country where such things were better managed.

Such a course seemed to Ross unwise to say the least of it. To be jolting broken bones over miles of inferior roads could do them no good at all. At the same time, he knew his brother-in-law—and that gentleman's obstinacy. If he was set on returning home, return he would. It might be possible, reflected his lordship to bring him by sea to Harwich, if weather conditions were reasonable. That would reduce the road travel considerably, and if they had to wait about for favourable winds, so much the better. The thought of travelling overland from Copenhagen to Calais and then taking ship to Dover was really out of the question under the circumstances.

Yes. That was what he would arrange. It never occurred to him to deny Elizabeth's appeal, nor did it enter his head that her return to England would suit him very nicely. He was simply concerned with the best way of managing an awkward business.

He pulled the bell for Bosworth. "And not a word of your errand to any one," he warned the courier. "There's no point in having the children on the fret for their father." The young man, who was one of Sir John's secretaries, nodded comprehension and went off with Bosworth to remove the dust of his journeying and partake of suitable refreshment, after which he rejoined his lordship in the library.

He found him just sealing a note which was addressed to Miss Ashley. It advised her briefly of his forthcoming absence and the reason for it, recommended her to keep the children in ignorance of their father's mishap, though this decision he would leave with her, and begged her, as a personal favour, to undertake the conduct of the household during his absence.

"I have complete faith in your judgement," he wrote. "I shall instruct Bosworth that they are all to take their orders from you. And you are the only person who knows where or why I am going. I would expect to be away for several weeks, since I cannot desert my sister until her affairs are running smoothly again. This means that you will have to see Benedict off to school. I am sorry for it, but Elizabeth's needs come first. Bid Dominic farewell for me. I shall hope to see him on my return."

He scrawled his initials at the end of this missive, sealed it, and turned to the waiting courier.

"Are you returning directly, or have you further business in this country?"

"Direct, milord. I thought to lie overnight in Town and then make for Dover. The overland route is likely to be quicker than the sea passage from Harwich, and her ladyship may have further need of my services."

"I think you could serve her better by taking passage in my yacht to Copenhagen. True, Swallow is lying in Southampton and you might have a long beat up channel if the wind does not favour you, but I shall need her in Copenhagen in any case to ensure the greatest possible degree of comfort for Sir John if he cannot be persuaded to rest quietly until his bones are mended. And Swallow certainly has the heels of any cross-channel packet. What do you say? If you are agreeable I will write you a note for Captain Brenchley and he will give you passage to Copenhagen. I myself will travel by Dover and Calais, which, as you say, is like to be quicker, and will be with Lady Elizabeth before you, I trust. But you should not be too far behind me. If you explain to Captain Brenchley that your business is urgent, I do not think that you will find him loitering. He will make all speed that the wind permits. Are you a good sailor, Mr Hughes?"

Mr Hughes grinned disarmingly and said that he was at least an enthusiastic one. It was plain that the prospect of a comfortable, if protracted, voyage in his lordship's luxuriously appointed yacht was very much to his taste, and since his conscience was appeased by the knowledge that Lord Valminster himself was hastening to his sister's side, he was only too happy to fall in with the suggestion.

His lordship scrawled a few lines for Captain Brenchley and bade Mr Hughes farewell, thanking him for his services and adding that if at any future time he could be of assistance to him, he would be happy to oblige. A gratified young man set out on the road to Southampton, while his lordship directed his man to put up such gear as he would require for an absence of several weeks and summoned Bosworth once more.

"I have no time to tell you the whole. I have writ it all down in this note for Miss Ashley, and I have no doubt she will admit you to her confidence. I am leaving the household in her charge while I am away, and am confident that you will render her all the assistance within your power."

He handed the note to Bosworth, who laid it solemnly on the low oak bench that stood in the hall. Miss Ashley could not miss seeing it there as soon as she and the children returned from the riding picnic that had marked the last day of the holidays.

Presently he saw master and man mount into the light travelling chaise. No further than London, he calculated thoughtfully, else it had been the coach, and a team rather than a pair. But where could the master be bound in such haste? For the first time since he had risen to his present eminence, Bosworth's information was incomplete. And to be dependent on Miss Ashley for its completion! He *liked* Miss Ashley, but here were signs and portents that required much pondering. *Could* it be that, at long last, his lordship was thinking of marriage? Bosworth knew him well enough to be sure that he would not commit the care of his household to any one whom he did not hold in the highest esteem. In such a case it behoved even a butler to tread warily.

Unfortunately he was so preoccupied in mulling over this amazing possibility that he failed to close the door leading to the kitchen

quarters. Dandy—the puppy selected by Adam
and Bridget as their choice from the rather
heterogeneous litter produced by a misalli-
ance between the gardener's spaniel and a
neighbouring collie, was prompt to discover
this omission and pushed the door further
ajar with an inquisitive nose. Dandy was
bored. His own especial humans had deserted
him for the whole of the day, and no one else
had time to play with him. He trotted out
into the hall and looked about him hopefully
for entertainment. The front door bell rang
and he advanced importantly to answer it.
Bosworth did not notice him. The vicar had
called to see his lordship, hoping to enlist his
interest in furthering the musical education
of one of the choir boys who, apart from having an exceptional voice, also showed some
talent for composition. But upon learning
that his lordship was away from home he
decided that the appeal would keep until his
return and took his leave after one or two
affable exchanges with Bosworth.

A playful little breeze blew through the
open door, fluttering the missive that lay on
the bench so that it set up a gentle pattering
sound. To a puppy's quick eyes and ears, here
was invitation. Bosworth was scarcely back
in his own sanctum before a moist black nose
was investigating the possibilities of this
strange leaf. It was larger and heavier than

the leaves which fell from the trees. He was
accustomed to playing endless chasing games
with those. This smelled quite different, but
it might have some entertainment to offer.

At first it was rather unsatisfactory. It did
not float and whirl away as the garden leaves
did—just flopped on the floor and lay still.
Very dull. He growled at it, but it did not
take up the challenge. He set one sturdy paw
on it and tugged at a corner with sharp little
teeth. It made a lovely noise as it tore, which
encouraged him to repeat the assault until
he had it in a wet mass of unrecognisable
shreds. Then he decided that it tasted rather
unpleasant after all and trotted off to seek
new distractions. Henry, passing through the
hall some ten minutes later, saw the mess,
remarked dispassionately, "That dratted pup
again," and deposited the remains in the fire
that burned winter and summer alike in the
hall fireplace. He wondered vaguely what the
pup had chewed up but did not think the incident worthy of mention to his superior.

Eight

The disappearance of the letter was discovered
upon the return of the picnic party. Bosworth
came forward in stately fashion to draw Miss
Ashley's attention to it, and stared in disbelief at the empty space where it should have
been. Briefly he explained the circumstances
to the lady in an under-voice, stressing the
importance of the missive in view of his lordship's hasty departure, and declaring that it
must be found. When prolonged search failed
to discover the important document, enquir-
ies were instituted and Dandy's activities
were revealed. Henry was perfectly frank
about his part in the affair, assuring his audience that, "No one wouldn't never have

known that it was a letter. Just a handful of soggy scraps with never a sign of writing on it."

Bosworth, with every wish in the world to find a scapegoat for what he felt to be his own negligence, could not honestly blame the lad for his action, and it was certainly of no help to blame the marauding puppy. Miss Ashley very sensibly said that the letter was gone and there was small use in fretting over its disappearance. Could Bosworth make any suggestions as to his lordship's possible destination or the duration of his absence from home? Unfortunately Bosworth was unacquainted with Mr Hughes who had not been very long in Sir John Browning's service, so he was unable to venture any surmise. He could only say that a young gentleman had called to see his lordship, a Mr Hughes, driving in a hired chaise; and that his lordship, after conferring with the visitor, had made hurried preparations for his own departure. He was able to add that the hired chaise had then left for Southampton, since he had chanced to hear Mr Hughes giving directions to the postilion, but this piece of information did not seem to shed any light on his lordship's movements. He repeated his lordship's parting remarks with great solemnity, assuring Miss Ashley that he and Mrs Palmer would give loyal support to the authority vested in her during his lordship's absence.

Miss Ashley, considerably startled by her sudden access of responsibility, said that she could only trust that that absence would be of very brief duration; that she would rely entirely upon the Earl's trusted servants to keep her informed as to the customary practices of the household, of which she was lamentably ignorant and that she took it that his lordship's delegation of authority referred rather to the management of his young relatives than to the conduct of domestic matters. Which showed, as Bosworth pointed out to Mrs Palmer, a very proper attitude, but was not what his lordship had said. Mrs Palmer nodded portentously. It was comforting to know that Miss Ashley put a proper value on their support, but she, for one, would be quite content to leave any awkward decisions to the young lady.

A week passed. Miss Ashley was not called upon to make any dramatic decisions. The great household continued to run on oiled wheels. Its new head disclaimed any desire to take over the planning of menus, assuring a very correct Mrs Palmer that she had only one complaint to make about the meals at Valminster, and adding, before the housekeeper could ruffle up, "They are too tempting by half. If I yielded to inclination I should grow as fat as poor Mrs Bennet." Since Mrs Bennet, the lodge keeper's wife, was of such massive proportions that she wheezed as she walked, only walked when it was essential, and needed—or so her husband declared— *both* leaves of the lodge gates opened before she could pass in or out, while Miss Ashley was slim as a willow, even a little too thin to suit fashionable demands, this was obviously complimentary. Mrs Palmer permitted herself a prim smile for the pleasantry and decided that there was no immediate threat to her customary sway.

Bosworth dealt diplomatically with callers, explaining that the Earl had been called away suddenly; that they were not sure of his exact whereabouts but were expecting to hear from him shortly; and that in any matter concerning the welfare of the tenants' families, Miss Ashley was empowered to act for her employer.

That caused one or two startled glances. Governesses were not usually so privileged. But the account of the adventure of the Cavern Fall was already part of the folk lore of the neighbourhood. Sensible people reckoned that Miss Ashley was a cut above the general run of governesses. Her dealings with such minor matters as were brought to her for adjustment did nothing to contradict this impression. She was obviously interested.

She was practical, but she was kind and human. She could sometimes make the chronic grumblers laugh at themselves—no small achievement—and generally arrange a satisfactory compromise between contending parties. In the farms and the cottages they talked about the new order—*how* they talked! But on the whole the comments were approving.

The children were rather disgruntled over his lordship's abrupt departure, the boys especially so, but the shadow of school lay over both Dominic and Benedict and their complaints were more subdued than they might otherwise have been. Moreover Graine made representations to Mr Oliver—his lordship's steward—which produced a very satisfactory tip to help soften the rigours of the academic groves to Benedict's untried feet. She herself attended to Dominic's needs in this direction. His lordship would undoubtedly have dealt with the matter had he been present, but although she was perfectly well aware of this she preferred to be independent. She smiled a little, thinking how his lordship would scold when he discovered what she had done, and when Dominic tentatively mentioned Christmas and hinted at the possibility of a short visit to Valminster, she did nothing to depress his hopes. The Earl might well invite him to bear Benedict company even if she herself was no longer a member of his household. After all, by Christmas she might well be established in Lady Elizabeth's town house or perhaps at Mounsell Park or even in Copenhagen.

For some odd reason these several alternatives, which at the beginning of her employment with the Brownings had seemed excitingly attractive, no longer held much appeal. All she really wanted was to go on living at Valminster, preferably with Dominic coming to share the holidays. For the summer had been quite delightful. Rather guiltily she recognised that she had been treated more as a guest than a servant, her share in every expedition carefully planned for her, her seat in the carriage always the most comfortable one. And now, of course, she was being thoroughly spoiled by her new authority. Small wonder that she did not want to leave Valminster, where at the moment she enjoyed all the consequences of the châtelaine. Firmly she applied herself to the task of correcting Bridget's French exercises.

Bereft of Dominic and Benedict the schoolroom party was rather subdued. Graine tried to devise one or two small treats for them but her own spirits were unaccountably low. She was missing the lively company of the boys, she told herself, and tried to suppress a tendency to wonder where his lordship was and how much longer it would be before he came home, though it was perfectly natural that she should be concerned, of course, since her responsibility would end with his return. She would miss that, too, she thought ruefully. It was exhilarating to have a finger in so many Valminster pies. Not since her father had died and Ashley House and the farms and stables and horses had all had to be sold to pay his debts, had she enjoyed such a varied and stimulating existence. For a moment she even toyed with the thought of seeking a post as a housekeeper rather than as a governess, but it was quite ineligible, she knew. She was too young, too pretty. And she had finished with playacting. Once was enough!

Her thoughts strayed again to a certain absent gentleman. Even though it meant her own relegation to the schoolroom world once more, she would be glad to see him come home. She had missed him more than she would have believed possible.

So. Now the truth was out. Not until he went away had she realised how much she had come to depend on him; had come—be honest, Graine—to care for him. He had worn so much the air of a slightly quizzical but indulgent elder brother to them all. She had been only vaguely aware how much all their comfort and enjoyment depended on him. She or Benedict or Bea had only to suggest some excursion, and everything was arranged for them. Milord chose horses for them to ride or carriages to drive in; he knew the best road to take, even the best days for visiting various places. To be sure he had servants a-plenty to carry out his orders; to go ahead and see that refreshment was awaiting them in a private parlour at some country inn. But his was the hand on the reins. Graine had known herself fortunate. It was rare, in her experience, for the gentleman of the house to concern himself with such trivial matters as schoolroom picnics.

It was only now that she realised how much her own enjoyment had depended on his society. While the children explored and sketched or climbed or fished in some brook as the fancy took them, their elders idled and talked. Graine would report some small success that one of the youngsters had achieved, or tell of some comical thing that had happened; his lordship might comment favourably on the improvement in Adam's horsemanship. But somehow, gradually, the talk would drift into a reminiscent vein. His lordship would remember travels abroad, and vow sincerely enough that he had never seen a countryside the equal of England in early summer. Graine must perforce insist that Ireland was superior. The grass was greener, the air softer and sweeter. Then they would both chuckle contentedly and fall silent for a while, only to begin again. There was nothing private or intimate about their talk. The other members of the party would wander up from time to time with some tale to tell or some trophy to be exhibited. Small wonder, thought Graine disgustedly, that she had not realised that she was falling in love. One did not expect something so important as love to arrive so unobtrusively. It had taken her by surprise, outflanked her defences. The one man who had assured her of her complete immunity from his attentions had stolen her heart; filched it away without sound or fuss, she thought, almost indignantly.

The turmoil of her feelings served to distract her for a little while from the bleakness of the future, but inevitably the time came when realisation was forced upon her. Two facts emerged. However much she might have come to value his lordship, he had nothing to offer her but kindness and consideration. She knew—only too well—how gentlemen behaved when their affections were engaged. Lord Valminster showed none of the symptoms. She quite forgot the promise he had given her and underestimated his iron self-control. But even if he had shown signs of succumbing to her attractions, such a match was so unequal as to seem ludicrous. To be sure, her birth was as good as his. Perhaps better, suggested a flare of pride, since the blood of ancient Irish kings ran in her veins. But the Earl was a great gentleman with vast holdings, not only in this country but in Jamaica. He moved in the highest social circles, and although he did not devote all his attention to politics his voice carried considerable weight when serious topics were discussed. Such a man was unlikely to consider an alliance with the daughter of the ramshackle, penniless Ashleys.

The other undeniable truth that struck her forcibly was the realisation that the less she saw of his lordship, the better it would be for her peace of mind. A continuation of the easy intercourse which they had enjoyed throughout the summer would do nothing to cure her infatuation. It was a depressing thought. She took what comfort she could from the knowledge that at the moment there was nothing she could do about it. In fact simple loyalty insisted that until he returned she must devote her best endeavours to guarding his lordship's interests. Like any other girl in love she found this a satisfactory prospect.

Three weeks elapsed before they had any word of his lordship. By that time, Graine, at any rate, was more than a little anxious. The letter was brief and business-like. By the time that she received it the writer expected to be on his way home. It had proved impossible to keep Sir John in check any longer, though he was really making very good progress despite his distrust of foreign doctors. If she had not yet told the children of his accident it was now perfectly safe to do so, since there seemed to be every prospect of his making an excellent recovery. Together with Sir John and Lady Elizabeth and their personal servants he hoped to leave Copenhagen in 'Swallow' in two days' time, bound for Harwich. From Harwich they would travel in Sir John's town coach—more capacious than his—but would she ask Oliver to arrange that his own coach, with the team of greys, should also be awaiting them upon arrival, to accommodate the rest of the party. It was impossible to give an exact time for their arrival at Harwich. So much depended on the wind. Perhaps ten days. It was unlikely to be less, but better to keep horses and servants idling about in Harwich for a day or so than keep Sir John waiting once he had reached his native shores. It would be difficult enough to persuade him to make the journey to Town in easy stages. They need not look for his own arrival at Valminster for at least another ten days after that, since he must see his sister and her husband safely installed in their own home and going along prosperously before he would be free to attend to his own affairs. He hoped that the children were well and be-

having themselves, and trusted that Miss
Ashley was not worn out with the care of a
large household which he had so unceremon-
iously thrust upon her. He had not thought
it would be for so long a time, but he would
make his apologies in due form when he saw
her again. Meanwhile he begged her to, "Go
on holding the castle for me."

The turn of phrase, with its hint of old cus-
toms, its reminder of women who had in every
truth held castles for their absent lords from
Crusading times to the Cromwellian wars,
touched Graine's imagination. She would indeed do that, she vowed, and no suggestion
that the price in personal suffering might be
a high one should prevent her.

She found Mr Oliver in the estate office
and disclosed to him the news conveyed in
the letter, together with the instructions
about the coach and greys, and then went in
search of Mrs Palmer and Bosworth. They
had served her in the kindliest fashion in
obedience to an order that must have seemed
very strange to them. It was their right to
hear news of the Earl at the first possible
moment.

They listened with grave interest while she
read aloud the main part of the letter, Mrs
Palmer commenting thoughtfully that bones
didn't mend so quickly when a gentleman
was in his middle years and that Sir John

would have to go carefully for several weeks yet. Bosworth was more concerned with the wider aspects of the situation. "Then that was what Mr Hughes was going to Southampton for," he announced triumphantly. "To carry a message to Captain Brenchley about taking Swallow over to Copenhagen," and much pleased with the acuteness of his own reasoning, ventured to suggest that they should send the chariot to Harwich as well as the coach. Likely Sir John and Lady Elizabeth would have a lot of heavy baggage, he pointed out, and then there would be Sir John's man and her ladyship's maid.

Graine said that she would put the suggestion to Mr Oliver, and went off to do so, leaving the pair happily talking over the news to which they had just been made privy and agreeing that it would be good to have his lordship home again. "Though I'm not saying that we haven't gone on very comfortably with Miss Ashley," concluded Mrs Palmer, with a benevolence induced by the fact that proper deference had been paid to her standing in the household.

Bosworth nodded sagely, and kept his own counsel about the amazing suspicion that had crossed his mind when first he heard of the Earl's dispositions.

Nine

His lordship, upon his return, found his young relatives deeply preoccupied with the manufacture of gifts for 'poor, dear Papa', designed to cheer his convalescence and assure him of their affection. Beatrice was hemming handkerchieves, Bridget embroidering a nightcap. Adam, fired by Benedict's success with Bea's workbox, was labouring over a collection of slats of wood which the Earl thought was a rat trap but which his nephew told him pityingly was a book rest, designed to hold Papa's book for him if he wished to read in bed. The Earl strongly suspected that its collapsible legs would collapse when least required to do so, while the tongue of wood designed to hold the book in place would certainly obscure half the printed page if it did not make it impossible to turn it. Nevertheless he felt pretty sure that Sir John would be pleased to receive this token of his son's regard, and did nothing to discourage the artisan.

Miss Ashley struck him as seeming rather subdued. Missing her brother, perhaps. Which reminded him that he had a crow to pluck with her on Dominic's account.

"I see from Oliver's accounts of expenditure that you sent Benedict off handsomely inlaid—and your brother penniless," he charged her, and she bit back a smile for the accuracy of her own prediction. "You must have known that I meant to tip him handsomely. You seem to have read my wishes to a nicety in all other respects. Why select your brother to be the one exception?"

"Because I did not choose to be generous at your expense," she told him coolly. "And he was not penniless. I provided for him quite adequately out of the handsome salary that your sister pays me. If you wish to tip him, it is no affair of mine."

He shook his head at her. "Your reasoning is at fault, Miss Ashley. On this one occasion it *was* your affair to be the interpreter of my wishes. You must learn to curb that flaring pride of yours. It distorts your judgement."

She was silent, acknowledging some justice in the rebuke.

He said swiftly, "And it ill beseems me to be ripping up at you for that one very understandable slip when I stand so deeply in your debt. You will think me the most ungrateful wretch alive, and I am most truly grateful though I do not quite see how I am to prove it to you. Especially as I am about to impose further on your good nature."

She looked at him enquiringly.

"My sister has asked me if I will keep the children with me, possibly until Christmas," he told her curtly. "I am aware that a prolonged residence under my roof will be distasteful to you. You have no doubt been counting the weeks until you can join the Brownings in Town, where there are shops and theatres and concerts to brighten your leisure—of which, in any case, you have had singularly little. But I am asking you to consent to this change of plan. Sir John—Sir John is the best of good fellows, but not the most even tempered. Especially in his present state. My sister feels that three lively youngsters cooped up in a house that is none too large might be rather too much for him. What do you say?"

Graine looked at him steadily. "You appear to be under some sort of misapprehension, milord. There is no question of refusal. I must naturally go with the children wherever their parents choose. But I shall be well content to remain at Valminster. Far from being distasteful to me, I have been very happy here; happier than I have been since my father died. To be sure there are no theatres or picture galleries—except your own—but you cannot say that we have lacked entertainment. It has certainly been quieter since the boys left but if the other three are to stay until Christmas I can foresee great preparations to be made. We shall not be dull, I promise you."

That promise was fulfilled. Gradually they slipped into a comfortable routine adapted to winter weather. Mornings were usually devoted to lessons, but if there was a meet within comfortable riding distance and the day was fine, they would sometimes ride out to see the start. On non-hunting days they rode or walked in the afternoons, returning ravenously hungry to an ample schoolroom tea, toasting bread or muffins over the fire, demolishing piles of bread and butter and jam and topping up with sticky gingerbread, jam tarts and plum cake. Very often the Earl would drop in on this cosy feast, arrogating to himself the post of toaster-in-chief, asking how their day had gone, relating something of his own activities. Occasionally he consulted Graine about such estate matters as

might be thought to lie within her understanding. Just so might a husband have
talked with a wife who was also a comrade.
She listened and answered equably, swallow-
ing the pain of his easy intimacy, never fal-
tering or wincing. Her self-control was admirable, matching his lordship's own. Perhaps
they stood upon terms unusually informal
between the master of the household and a
mere governess, but a listener would have
found nothing beyond shared interests and
a certain community of tastes between them.
His lordship never guessed that Graine was
longing quite as desperately as he was for the
day when she could decently quit his roof, if
for very different reasons, and Graine saw
only the behaviour of a very great gentleman
in the distinguishing attentions that he paid
her. She was a useful asset to the family, and
she knew that she had served his lordship
well during his absence abroad. It was like
him, she thought lovingly, that he should still
go out of his way to include her in the activities of the estate and not just push her aside
now that she was no longer really needed.
Her days were bitter-sweet. She rejoiced in
his nearness, in the brief snatches of his society that might come at any moment, trea-
sured his every word and gesture—and set
a rigid guard on her own demeanour so that
he should never suspect her secret. If that

should come to pass, she would die of shame, she thought. It would embarrass him so.

So matters stood between them when Lady Elizabeth wrote to her brother to suggest that the children might be permitted to pay a brief visit to their parents. She was longing to see them, she said, and Sir John, though still walking with a pronounced limp, was now able to pursue many of his normal activities. A visit of two or three days would allow her to assess how soon her family could be reestablished in their own home. Miss Ashley would no doubt be able to check any tendency to hang around their Papa too much, and a few days in Town would also afford *her* an opportunity of visiting her sister and that sister's new small son, her ladyship concluded kindly.

His lordship liked the scheme. It was the first step towards ending this interminable waiting. The children were enthusiastic about the prospect of an unexpected holiday but anxious that their plans for spending a riotous Christmas at Valminster should not be thwarted at this late date. Graine could not quite subdue a rise of the heart when the Earl announced that he himself would take the party in charge and see them safely to their destination.

Beatrice promptly seized the opportunity to remind him of an old promise to escort her to Vauxhall Gardens as soon as she should be old enough for such delights. With Miss Ashley to play propriety there could be no least objection. His lordship, however, pointed out that at this season of the year the gardens were closed—and then took pity on her disappointed face and said that if her Mama permitted perhaps he could take her to the play.

The visit was a great success. The children, a little overawed by a father who still leaned heavily on a cane, behaved with unusual decorum in his presence. The gifts so painstakingly prepared for him were well received, the neatness of the workmanship winning his commendation, and the schoolroom wing was sufficiently far removed from his apartments to prevent any possibility that good relations would be jeopardised by the incredible amount of noise created by two children and a lively puppy—for Dandy had accompanied the party to Town at the children's earnest request, and unlike his owners he was not in the least subdued by his new surroundings, taking exception to passing traffic, of which there was a good deal, and showing his disapproval by bursts of furious barking. It was fortunate that Lady Elizabeth, unwontedly indulgent in her pleasure at the reunion with her children, was sure that he would soon adapt to Town ways and learn to moderate his objections. She settled down to enjoy a comfortable cose with her elder daughter, assuring Graine that the abigail who waited on the school-room was perfectly to be relied upon to take charge of the children while she, Graine, visited her own sister, which she must be simply longing to do.

Graine took advantage of the permission. She was indeed eager to see Bridget and her first nephew, who turned out to be a plump and placid infant looking remarkably like his father. Her attempts to engage his attention were unavailing. He put his thumb in his mouth and presently went to sleep, leaving the sisters to an exchange of family news. It ended, as such family conferences so often do, in Bridget's voicing her disapproval of Graine's sober grey gown and severe hair style.

"Makes you look every day of thirty," she complained. "Next you'll be taking to caps."

Graine chuckled, taking this sisterly plain speaking in good part. "You're in the wrong of it there, Bridie my girl. I've just discarded them."

The whole story had to come out then, of course, and Bridget listened and laughed and was vastly intrigued. She understood in part the reasons that had driven her sister to such absurd lengths, but could only be thankful that the masquerade was no longer necessary. Her own marriage was not in the vein of high romance though she and her Vernon were very fond of each other, but like most married ladies she saw marriage as the best vehicle to bring fulfilment and contentment to any woman, and the thought that her lovely, spirited loveable little sister should live out all her years in spinsterhood, dependent on the whims of others for her livelihood, was not to be endured. Marriage, obviously, was the thing for Graine. But without a respectable portion it was not so simple to arrange, and no man would look twice at her in her present guise, thought Bridget crossly.

She had gathered that Graine's plans for the near future included a Christmas spent at Valminster. Also, and perhaps more important, that she was treated as one of the family, not just when they were alone but even when there were guests. One ought to make a push to take advantage of such opportunities. If only she were decently dressed she might well catch the eye of some discerning gentleman. He would probably think that she was an impoverished connection of the Valminster family, but that would do her no dis-service and could be amended later if anything came of such a chance acquaintance. She harked back to the question of suitable dress.

"I know you do not wish to hang on my sleeve, but surely you could permit me to buy you *one* decent gown. You know that I have ample pin money. Indeed, at the moment I am positively plump in the pocket, having spent very little these past few months. Could you not look upon it as a Christmas gift?"

But Graine shook her head. "You will need lots of new dresses yourself. I daresay you are heartily sick of the ones you had in the early stages of your pregnancy. And since I like to be beforehand with the world, I do not propose to spend my carefully hoarded guineas on dresses which I do not need. However, there are several gowns in the trunk that you are keeping for me. I judged them unsuitable for my situation, but we can look them over and see if there is anything that pleases your fastidious taste."

But only one of the dresses earned Bridget's approval. Most of them were shabby and outdated. The fortunes of the Ashleys had been at low ebb for a good many years. But Papa had somehow found the money for Bridget's wedding, and for a new dress for her sister. The dress, though three years old and not precisely fashionable, was as good as new and extremely becoming. Looking at herself in Bridget's tall mirror, Graine knew she could not resist the temptation to wear it if opportunity offered. Perhaps if they went to the theatre—or even for Christmas. It was rather too grand for every day use. But there could be no denying that the richness of the dark crimson damask suited her to admiration, accentuating the delicacy of her skin, while the square-cut neckline and close-fitting bodice gave her something of the air of a mediaeval princess. Yes. She would wear it. Once, just once, she would like someone—unspecified—to see her looking her very best.

"I'll take this one with me," she told the gratified Bridget. "Do you think it is too grand to wear at a theatre party?"

Bridget admitted judicially that the dress might be considered suitable for Covent Garden or Drury Lane, but was probably too grand for the lesser theatres. Graine hoped that Beatrice's tastes would incline towards serious drama, but privately rather doubted it.

In this supposition she proved to be entirely correct. Fortunately the Earl was at hand to rescue his niece from her dilemma. He suggested that the party should be enlarged to include Adam and Bridget and that they should all go to Sadler's Wells to see Dog Bruin in the Great Aquatic Drama, Philip and his Dog. Lady Elizabeth was dubious. Sadler's Wells was a home of melodrama, patronised by all the scaff and raff. Her brother assured her that the piece was unexceptionable. The main actor was the dog, who began by rescuing the infant child from a rushing torrent (with real water) into which the villain had thrown it, and ended by pursuing that evil character so closely that he obliged him to throw himself off a cliff into the waters of a great tank and then followed him into it, seized him by the throat and drowned him. Adam shivered ecstatically at the prospect of seeing such stirring events, and his mother had not the heart to deny him the treat, particularly when the Earl assured her that all the 'ton' were flocking to see the spectacle and that he would endeavour to secure a box, so that her precious little family should not be exposed to any danger of infection through coming into too close contact with London's unwashed. Since Beatrice unhesitatingly preferred the Dog Bruin to more improving works, the matter was settled to the satisfaction of everyone but Graine, who could not feel that her beautiful dress was appropriate to the occasion.

Sir John and Lady Elizabeth accepting the Earl's invitation to spend Christmas at Valminster, another problem was satisfactorily settled. The actual date on which the children would return to the parental roof was not finally agreed, but it was understood that it would be some time in January after Dominic and Benedict had returned to school. During his brief stay in London the Earl had found time to call on Sir Everard Hastings, and to

win his consent for Dominic's Christmas holidays to be spent at Valminster. Dominic's
self-appointed guardian was not loath. He
had thoroughly enjoyed his Roman tour in
the summer, and had quite seen the force of
his friend's argument about his god-son's
youth and energy. He could manage pretty
well when the boy was at school all day, but
there could be no denying that the holidays
were something of a problem. With every inclination to do his duty by Dominic, he was
happy to see the problem of the Christmas
holiday so comfortably solved. Dominic's own
delight was never in doubt. He came home
before his lordship took his leave, and his
pleasure was patent. A certain regrettable
omission was repaired, and Dominic, quite
unselfconscious, announced that now he could
manage Christmas gifts for every one and did
his lordship think that Adam would like a
guinea-pig? His lordship, wondering be-
musedly what gift was destined to come *his*
way, thought that Adam would be delighted,
wondered briefly what his sister would have
to say, and took his leave.

Ten

Christmas came and went. So far as Graine could judge, all her charges' hopes and expectations were fulfilled to the hilt. There was even an unexpected bonus in the form of a spell of cold weather immediately preceding the festival. It stopped hunting, of course, but it made possible the alternative joys of sledging, skating and snowballing. The novelty appealed to everyone. Where skating was concerned, the Earl and Beatrice were the experts. Graine's Irish childhood had offered few opportunities of acquiring the graceful art. She stumbled about happily enough with the children until his lordship took her in hand and skated with her. She was light and supple with an easy, natural balance and rhythm. With the strong, competent hands to guide and support her she soon began to catch the knack of the thing and to learn the exhilaration of swooping over the ice. It was a delightful sensation and left her flushed and breathless with sparkling eyes. It did nothing at all to allay the fierce longing that consumed her. A determined effort was needed to release her fingers from his lordship's clasp. They clung instinctively. Deprived of his support she faltered and almost fell, so that he caught her elbow and guided her to a rustic seat that had been set on the verge of the lake, kneeling to remove her skates and telling her firmly that she had done enough for one day.

"As with riding," he explained, "you use muscles that you did not know you possessed. If you over-do it, you will be painfully stiff tomorrow. The trouble is that these perfect conditions occur so rarely that everyone tends to do too much, because a thaw might set in at any time."

Dominic and Benedict, arriving the following week, took to the new pastime with zest, though Dominic was no more proficient than his sister, and even Lady Elizabeth was tempted on to the ice on several occasions, declaring happily that the exercise made her feel quite young and frivolous and not in the least like the mother of a promising family. When the early darkening drove them indoors they would play commerce or some such round game until bed time came for Adam and Bridget, the latter protesting because Benedict, only a few weeks older, was allowed to stay up later, benefiting from the latitude permitted to a schoolboy on holiday.

The house was full of secrets. There were suppressed giggles and the sounds of scurrying feet and rustling paper as gifts were privily displayed or hurriedly concealed. There was an expedition to the woods to bring home the yule log and the masses of holly and ivy that were needed to decorate the great hall. Cheerful young voices sang Christmas carols and his lordship permitted himself a small private dream. Some day it would not be just a brood of nephews and nieces—fond as he was of them. Some day the vast rooms would echo to the voices of *his* children. His—and Graine's. She was not indifferent to him, he felt sure. And given time and patient wooing, perhaps he could turn liking into the love that he so ardently desired.

The difficulty was that he had small inclination towards patience. Thanks to his sister's difficulties he had waited too long already. At thirty seven a man knew his own mind and wanted to make the most of the good years that were still left to him. The instincts of hospitality warred with the urgency of the lover and the lover won. He was thankful that the Christmas holiday was a short one, and hoped that John and Elizabeth would not linger on once the older boys had gone back to school. The sooner they removed their brood—and Graine—from Valminster, the sooner he would be freed from that infuriating promise that he would not press his attentions on the girl. A promise so lightly given, so maddeningly frustrating now.

He would give her a week, he decided. A week in which to accustom herself to the ways of his sister's house and to learn, he hoped, to miss him a little. Then he would post up to Town and try to reach an understanding with her. She was of age, so there were no guardians to placate, but it might be politic to call on the elder sister, Bridget. There were two older brothers, too, but both were overseas. Dominic's support he felt he could perfectly rely upon. It did not occur to him that both guardians and relatives with Graine's interests at heart would be likely to extend a cordial, even ecstatic, welcome to the Earl of Valminster, once they had assimilated the incredible fact that he had come a-wooing. Concerned only with the disparity in age between himself and his little love, he gave no thought to the social and financial advantages that he could offer her.

Graine wore her crimson dress for dinner on Christmas Day, a feast which was to take place at the old-fashioned dinner hour of three o'clock. The morning had been devoted to church-going and present giving, after which his lordship decreed a walk in the sharp frosty air to give them all appetites for the traditional fare that was to come. Adam was permitted to take his new sledge, on the strict understanding that the guinea-pig—a highly successful present—was left at home. Changing her dress after the expedition, her body glowing with the exhilaration of exercise and much shared laughter, Graine's mirror told her that she was looking her best, cheeks vivid, eyes alight with that speculative mischief that was so much a part of her personality that it had to be severely repressed during her masquerade. There was no doubt about it, she conceded ruefully. Clothes could do a good deal for a girl, even if she was passably good looking without adventitious aids.

Beatrice's eager praise of her appearance and Lady Elizabeth's kindly if more temperate approval served to endorse her own verdict, but unfortunately she was not privileged to see the Earl's first reaction. It so chanced that her attention was engaged by his sister when he came into the room. Lady Elizabeth was examining the pretty crystal beads that had been Dominic's gift to *his* sister, but she glanced up at Ross's entrance. Since she was facing him, she missed nothing; the sudden check, the eager look in his eyes, the one impetuous stride, the swift restraint. She looked sharply at the girl, so innocently displaying her new gaud, and recognised her complete unconsciousness of the effect that she had produced. For herself she found the situation vastly intriguing. Long ago she had stopped bringing lovely or charming females to his lordship's notice in the hope that he would drop the handkerchief to one of them, having come to the conclusion that he was not the marrying kind. It was a great pity, but she supposed that he preferred his freedom, and with Benedict to inherit there was no need to sacrifice it in order to ensure the succession. And now, at the age of thirty seven, he must needs fall in love with little Graine Ashley.

In the normal course of events, Lady Elizabeth would have considered such a choice most unsuitable. She had a good deal more regard for her brother's consequence than he had himself, and would have thought that he was throwing himself away in most lamentable fashion. A mere governess! But Graine was her dear friend Bridget's sister, which was rather different. She had no fortune, of course, but that was not an insuperable bar since the Earl had more than enough for two. Nor had her ladyship forgotten the signal service that the girl had rendered her in the adventure at the Cavern Fall. She was inclined to think that the match would do very well, and even began to plume herself on the notion that it had all come about through her. If she had not sent the children and their governess to Valminster, the two might never have met. Or if they had met they would not have been thrown so much into each other's society as was bound to happen in the country. She wondered why her brother had not declared himself. Some foolish notion of propriety, she supposed indulgently. It was true that Graine's position in a bachelor household *had* been rather a delicate one. But all that was at an end now that *she* was there to play duenna. And not even her modest-minded brother could suppose for a moment that the girl would hesitate over her answer. She would naturally jump at such a splendid opportunity of establishing herself. Settling comfortably to watch the charades that the children were to perform for them, her ladyship devoted her thoughts to consideration of how she could best forward her brother's courtship.

It would be a pity to take Graine back to Town before the business was satisfactorily concluded. There was no particular hurry for her own return, and John seemed quite content at present with the dawdling country way of life, while the children were probably happier at Valminster than they would be in Town. Her ladyship cast about in her mind for some excuse for prolonging her stay. She found one very conveniently in the weather. The cold spell came to an end. Heavy rainfall added to melting snow made travelling both hazardous and uncomfortable. No one who was not absolutely obliged to travel would do so, said Lady Elizabeth placidly, and she was sure that she could impose on her dear brother's hospitality for a little while longer. Her dear brother, seething with impatience at this further delay in his plans, assured her of his complaisance, and gilded the lily by reminding her that Valminster was her childhood home and that she must always regard it as still her home. Privately he trusted that, with the end of the holiday festivities and the children back in a regular routine of lessons, the depressing weather would soon drive Sir John and his wife to seek the solace of Town life to relieve their boredom.

It might well have done so. But he himself, albeit quite unwillingly, provided another reason for delay.

The uncertainty of his future had made him restless, and to add to his discomfort he was sleeping badly. This was a most unusual phenomenon and he scarcely knew how to deal with it. To be quacking himself with draughts and nostrums warranted to ensure sound sleep (and an amazing number of other benefits to the human system) was unthinkable. He fell into the habit of strolling in the park when sleep eluded him, often coming home soaked and weary in the small hours. On one such foray he ran foul of a party of poachers, who, their night's work successfully completed, were on their way home with a well filled sack. His lordship, whose mind was on matters far from rabbits and pheasants, halted for a moment, full in their path. Three of them tried to rush him, the fourth making off as rapidly as the heavy sack would permit.

In his Oxford days his lordship had been a notable exponent of the manly art. But that was some twenty years ago, and the care of his vast estates left little time for sparring practice. Nevertheless he dropped his first assailant with a right hook to the jaw. The other two drew off for a moment. There was a hoarse mutter of, "You go for 'is mark, George. I'll tackle 'im from the side."

His lordship mentally thanked them for the information and stood lightly balanced on the balls of his feet, awaiting the promised attack. He got in a heavy body blow on the frontal assailant, but the gentleman who had suggested attacking from the side used a knife, stabbing savagely at his victim's shoulder. It went deep, but fortunately slanted upwards, the Earl being considerably taller than his opponent. At the same moment his other attacker landed a blow on the temple that sent him dizzy and sprawling to measure his length on the turf while the poachers made good their escape.

It was some minutes before he recovered sufficiently to get to his feet. The wound in his shoulder was bleeding freely and there was nothing he could do to staunch the flow. His only course was to get back to the house as swiftly as possible and get help.

This he proceeded to do, but by the time he reached his goal he was weakening rapidly, sick and giddy from loss of blood. It was fortunate that the devoted Bosworth invariably waited up until his lordship came back from his night wanderings. After one shocked exclamation he was swift to set about mending matters. With the help of his lordship's man a pad was bound tightly over the ugly wound. It checked the bleeding. The patient was tenderly installed in a comfortable chair and the fire made up to guard against the danger of a chill, while rain-soaked clothing was peeled off and a warm dressing gown substituted. Bosworth heated wine, to which he surreptitiously added a generous measure of brandy, and coaxed his master to swallow the potent brew. The Earl was docile until the butler spoke of sending for the doctor. At this he roused himself to veto the suggestion. Time enough for that in the morning, he pronounced, and no need to drag the poor fellow from his bed at this hour of the night. Bosworth was dubious but allowed his judgement to be overruled. The master *did* look a mite better, he decided, with a trifle of colour creeping back into his cheeks; and he had never been a one for grand fusses about his health.

Lady Elizabeth took over the reins next morning. Apprised by Bosworth of the injury that her brother had sustained, she went straight to his room to find him very feverish and very uncomfortable. There was no more bleeding but the wound looked much inflamed, the flesh around it swollen and discoloured. The doctor must be summoned she decreed, and rated poor Bosworth for not having done this at once.

The doctor looked solemn. The wound had not touched any vital spot but it seemed possible that some portion of clothing had been driven into it. He ordered hot fomentations and a light diet, roundly condemned the administration of wine and spirits, and promised to send over a draught that would ease the patient's discomfort and help him to sleep.

In fact the Earl slept for most of the day, though his slumber was uneasy. The fomentations seemed to afford him a measure of relief. His condition gave no cause for serious anxiety, though it was obvious that he would need careful nursing for some days.

In the circumstances it was only natural that Lady Elizabeth should defer her return to Town yet again. Who else should tend her brother? It would hardly be proper for Graine to do so, and nothing, she told her husband, could take the place of a woman's touch in a sick-room. Nor was she willing to leave her brother to the care of servants, however devoted. Just see what had come of Bosworth's ministrations! Enough to cast any one into a high fever, the doctor had said.

In one respect, however, her kindly scheming failed. No suggestion of hers availed to win her brother's consent for Miss Ashley to visit the sick-room. Not even a week later when he was quite convalescent and might have been expected to enjoy a quiet game of piquet, or even having his visitor read to him. It was no part of Miss Ashley's duties to tend the sick, or even to entertain the convalescent, he said firmly. Lady Elizabeth could not understand his attitude, but she knew better than to go counter to his wishes. Miss Ashley enquired decorously after his progress each morning, and that was all the news she had of him, since the children, too, were excluded from his presence.

His lordship's reasoning was quite simple. It was bad enough to be ten years older than his love. He had no desire to play the invalid as well. At least he would offer her a man in the prime of his health and strength, not the sickly looking creature that he appeared at this present. But Graine felt the rebuff sharply. She had thought that at least she could count on his lordship's friendship.

She saw him once or twice before the Brownings eventually took their delayed departure, but only briefly and never alone. The fever had pulled him down a little. His face was thinner and paler, his stride lacked its old impulsive vigour and his manner was quieter, more restrained. She missed the old, teasing note and her heart was very tender towards him, but he seemed infinitely remote, grave and quiet. Together with the children she took a protracted farewell of Valminster, re-visiting all the places that had been so familiar, with never a thought that she would see his lordship again, save in the way of the occasional family visit.

Eleven

The interlude of a week which the Earl had planned was extended to three. Business which had accumulated during his illness must be attended to, and to his disgust he found that he still tired easily. A long day in the saddle left him exhausted. To complicate matters still further, the gang of poachers that had attacked him was apprehended during a raid on a neighbouring estate and he was invited to identify the man who had stabbed him and to give evidence at his trial; a distasteful duty, but a necessary one. He was thankful that the men were strangers to him, part of a band of tinkers who wandered the countryside, accomplished thieves and highway robbers. The honest folk who had suffered from their depredations for many months would be thankful when the sentence of transportation was carried out. There were some who grumbled that it should have been a hanging matter. A man might pick up the odd bird on a dark night, knowing the risk he ran, but an organised raid was a different matter and there was no call to have used a knife. Public sympathy was on the side of his lordship, who was held to have behaved with foolish generosity in not pressing a charge of attempted murder.

Graine was making a conscientious attempt to find a measure of contentment in her situation. She knew that she was singularly fortunate. Her employer was kind and considerate, her charges were genuinely fond of her and gave no trouble. She could scarcely have been better placed. What ailed her, then, that she should be so low-spirited? She made determined efforts to enjoy the amenities that were available. The London scene was not new to her. On previous visits she had found it stimulating and amusing. Though she had a natural preference for country life she also enjoyed theatres and concerts and assemblies, not to mention the endless delights of the shops. She had often dreamed of spending a Season in London when all these delights were not strictly limited by her slender purse. Now here she was, for once beforehand with the world, since there had been nothing to spend her money on during the months she had passed at Valminster. It was disheartening to discover that now, when she could afford some of the small luxuries for which she had so often yearned, they had lost their appeal. She bought a handsome silver-gilt mug for her new nephew, but took no interest in the delightful fripperies designed for personal adornment. She came to the conclusion that work was the best anodyne for an aching heart and spent her leisure with the children, amusing them and playing with them when lessons were done until even Lady Elizabeth declared that never were children so much indulged, and that she really must insist that Graine have *some* time to herself. But for one reason or another the various schemes never came to fruition and Graine continued to spend her free time in the schoolroom. Evenings, with Adam and Bridget both asleep, were the worst times, for Beatrice was frequently in the drawing room, learning how to make herself conversable among the wide range of guests whom her parents had entertained at dinner. Often the girl would run up to Graine for a comfortable gossip before bed-time, telling whom she had met and what they had said. Sometimes her mother detained her and she would go straight to bed. In either case there were long hours to be got through when reading—even poetry and novels—failed to hold her attention; when sewing seemed a burden, and she could not think of any letters that must be written. She would drift over to the battered schoolroom pianoforte and allow her fingers to wander idly over its keys. Sometimes she would sing softly to herself, wistful Irish airs that her nurse had crooned to the baby Graine, airs that had no words but a burden of aching sorrow. Sometimes she would find herself fitting words to the music. They were words of love and loss and grief. They were a sign that it was time to be done with wallowing in self-pity. Time to think of tomorrow, and to go to bed.

She scarcely noticed the shy attentions of Mr Hughes. Sir John's young secretary had been swift to note the attractions of the new addition to the household. Sometimes he managed to contrive an errand so that he could accompany the schoolroom party on their walk. Graine received his overtures of friendship civilly and forgot him within minutes of his departure. Only once did she show any sign of animation, and that was when he chanced to mention Lord Valminster's yacht, 'Swallow', speaking enthusiastically of his voyage to Copenhagen. Sailing seemed to him an odd interest for a female, but he was well aware that this was the first time that he had really engaged her attention. He made the most of it, expounding at length on 'Swallow's' best points of sailing with a wealth of technical jargon that took his listener well out of her depth. She listened patiently, finding some small comfort from this tenuous link with his lordship.

Considerably encouraged, Mr Hughes said that he would very much like Miss Ashley to make the acquaintance of his mother. She was a widow, residing in Kensington. It was not too far to drive if Miss Ashley had a free afternoon, and Sir John had given him permission to use the light chaise if no one else needed it. Not a very dashing vehicle, perhaps, but a prudent choice for a time of year when the weather was notoriously unreliable.

Graine heard the wistful note in the pleasant voice, and awoke to the delicacy of her position. Mr Hughes, she guessed, would very much have liked to invite her to drive in some dashing, sporting vehicle of his own. Her senses were alerted to a new source of embarrassment, but the young man had been kind and courteous. She did not wish to hurt him by a direct snub, the more so since her own stupid heedlessness, her preoccupation with her personal problems, had led her into offering what could only be regarded as encouragement. She thanked Mr Hughes for his kindly thought and was sure she would much enjoy such a meeting as he suggested, but she could see no immediate prospect of a free afternoon. In this she maligned an employer who kept urging her to make better use of her free time, but desperate cases demanded stern measures. To visit Mr Hughes's mother might well lead to a degree of intimacy between them which she did not desire, encourage hopes that must wither and die painfully. She would not do it. Better to disappoint him now, even if Lady Elizabeth must bear an unfair share of the blame.

In the event it was her brother Dominic who established his claim on her free afternoon, and Lady Elizabeth who insisted that he do so. Dominic and her ladyship had reached easy terms over the Christmas holidays. The boy had not hesitation in calling upon her and asking if he might speak with his sister, adding, when an abigail had gone to summon Graine, that there was nothing particularly private in his business, and if her ladyship could spare the time he would be glad of her opinion as well as Graine's.

The father of one of his school friends had offered him a position in his London counting house when the time came for him to leave school. Mr Sutcliffe was an East India merchant and also controlled wide shipping interests. His own son, Evan, Dominic's friend, was destined to follow his father into the business, but he was an only son, and Mr Sutcliffe felt that he had room for *two* reliable apprentices. Dominic would have everything to learn, but if he worked hard he could rely on steady promotion. It was an excellent opening for a likely lad. Mr Sutcliffe's reputation for integrity and fair dealing stood high. Uncle Everard thought Dominic very fortunate to be offered such an opportunity. Bridie was enthusiastic. To be sure there had never been an Ashley in trade before, she said, but that was fusty old prejudice, and for her part she thought that it was high time that one of the family made some money. The East Indian trade was the place to do it. In twenty years' time Dominic would be a wealthy Nabob, able to offer his patronage to his own young nephew.

What did Graine think?

Graine shook her head doubtfully. It was easy for Uncle Everard and Bridie to talk. They were kind enough and certainly had Dominic's interests at heart. But both were comfortably circumstanced and neither had ever had to earn a living. Graine knew something of the drudgery of routine, the weariness induced by conscientious application to a job for which one had no natural liking. If Dominic had a fancy for the Indian trade or for shipping concerns, it was a different matter. In that case his life would be a busy and contented one. If it was prosperous as well, so much the better. But she would not willingly see him apprenticed to a trade that he detested, be the prospects never so golden.

"What do you think about it yourself?" she probed, and was swift to see the shadow of doubt on his face.

"I should like working with Evan. We get along pretty well together. And later on, Mr Sutcliffe says, there will be a chance to travel. His idea is that once we know our work we could take over the Calcutta office. I should like that. But to be spending all my days on an office stool, making entries in ledgers and studying profit and loss—well—I just don't know. I don't suppose it'd be so very different from school. And if I found it dull and boring I don't know if I would work hard enough to satisfy Mr Sutcliffe. At school I always did best at the subjects that I enjoyed."

He had touched the core of Graine's own doubts. Lady Elizabeth said shrewdly, "If you were entirely free to choose, what would you like to do?"

His answer was prompt. "Something that took me out of doors a good deal. Probably to do with farming or horse breeding, like Papa. Not racing. It's the animals that appeal to me, not the excitement of a race course."

"Not book work," said Lady Elizabeth reflectively.

"Well actually there's quite a bit of book work to do with breeding horses. Or any other animals, come to that. You have to know the blood lines and keep careful records. But I like *that* sort of book work. And Mr Oliver showed me some of the book work that goes to the running of Valminster when I was there in the summer, and I liked that, too."

Silence fell, while the three of them contemplated such a life as Dominic described and the one that was offered to him. The difference was vast.

A plan began to form itself in Lady Elizabeth's mind. It was only loosely connected with the problem of Dominic's future, though it should prove helpful in that respect, too. But as regards a certain project of her own, she felt that it might well prove to be a master stroke.

"Ross is the man to advise you in such a case," she announced, with an air of decision that brooked no argument. "Sir John would certainly side with Sir Everard and Bridie. The financial prospects would out-weigh the years of drudgery. Besides, *he* likes poring over musty old papers and arguing over clauses and premises. He would see nothing wearisome in the life that Mr Sutcliffe suggests for you. In fact he would probably find a fatal fascination in cargo manifests and bills of lading. Ross will take a more dispassionate view, and since many of his tastes seem to agree with Dominic's, he may even be able to suggest some form of employment that would be more suitable."

Dominic's face brightened considerably, but Graine viewed her employer with a wary eye.

"You shall go down to Valminster this very day," planned her ladyship briskly. "No use dilly-dallying. I daresay Mr Sutcliffe will want your decision pretty soon, Dominic. You may take my town carriage. I shall not need it today. The roads are reasonably dry, so you should encounter no particular difficulty and should be back by nightfall. In any case there is a moon, so long as the clouds hold off. And you shall take your sister with you. No, don't argue, Graine. I am sure I have been saying for ever that you are wearing yourself to a shred over those abominable brats of mine. You shall have an afternoon of holiday, and you may discuss your brother's plans at leisure during the drive. Bear my greetings to *my* brother and tell him it is high time he paid us another visit. Now run up to your room and put on a carriage dress and a warm pelisse. The evenings are still cold."

Graine did as she was bid, half reluctant, half eagerly. Lady Elizabeth turned to Dominic, her glance assessing him thoughtfully. A likeable lad, sensible and tactful. She would trust him.

"Will you do something for me, Dominic?"

"Very willingly," he assured her.

She considered for a moment, then said slowly, "I think that my brother might like to have private speech with Graine. You will understand that there may be possibilities that he does not care to disclose before you for fear of raising unfounded hopes. If opportunity offers, leave them alone together."

The uncomplicated Dominic saw nothing strange in the request. "Of course, ma'am. I quite understand," he was telling her, as Graine came into the room dressed for the journey.

They were so fortunate as to find his lordship at home and free to receive them immediately, a little surprised at this unexpected visit but friendly and welcoming. He had, in fact, been toying with the notion of paying his sister a visit at the end of the week and contemplating with some dismay the difficulties that would stand in the way of getting Graine to himself for even a few minutes during such a visit. This unheralded arrival struck him as clear evidence of the intervention of providence. It must be put to good use.

He listened attentively while Dominic explained the reason for their visit and shyly apologised for taking up his time.

"It was at Lady Elizabeth's suggestion that we came to consult you," he finished. "She even lent us her own carriage. She was sure that you would know just what I should do. What do you think, sir? Ought I to accept Mr Sutcliffe's offer?"

The Earl shook his head. "It is not a matter to be decided lightly," he said soberly. "A man's work is the most important thing in his life. It should be chosen carefully, with a view to making the best of his talents and abilities. Do you think that such work as Mr Sutcliffe offers you will do that?"

Dominic looked solemn. "I don't think I *have* any particular talents," he said ruefully. "I'm not above average clever with my books, but Mr Sutcliffe said that wouldn't matter so long as I could remember what I was shown. I can do *that*, I think. And he was very keen about honesty and industry. I don't know so much about those because I've never been tested very high. I'm honest, I hope. But it might not be so easy to stick to one's work industriously in a climate like Calcutta's."

"An answer that seems to allay any doubts I might have felt about your honesty," returned the Earl drily. "Look, Dominic. Leave it with me for a day or two. I would like to take more time to think about it. As you say, it is an excellent opening for the right stamp of lad, but somehow I don't quite see you wearing out an office stool for the next ten or fifteen years. Something more active, I should have thought."

Dominic sighed. "Uncle Everard thinks I should accept," he confessed. "He says I can go on living with him, as it will be quite convenient for the City."

"That is very obliging of him," said his lordship. "But while I hold him in considerable respect for his scholarship, he is what I would describe as an indoor man. I doubt if he understands your leaning to an active open air occupation, which *I* feel to be more in your line than office work. But as I said, it is an important decision and not one to be hurried. Let me see if I can come up with any alternative suggestion before you make up your mind."

Dominic was very willing. He turned to the delicate business of ensuring that the Earl had a chance of discussing the business privately with his sister, as Lady Elizabeth had suggested. On the journey to Valminster he had debated and rejected half a dozen excuses for leaving the pair alone, and had been almost in despair of achieving anything credible when it suddenly struck him that he had a perfectly legitimate and truthful reason. When he had gone back to school after the holiday, Mrs Palmer had presented him with a large plum cake with which to allay the pangs of hunger created by too much study. She would like to hear about the feast that he had shared with his cronies, and to know how much the fellows had enjoyed her bounty. This he now explained to his host, asking if he might run up to the housekeeper's room and tell her about it.

"By all means," returned his lordship, with perhaps rather more enthusiasm than the simple suggestion merited. "And you might ask her to order some refreshment for you and your sister before you set out for Town. Something fairly substantial, tell her, because I doubt if you will get home in time for dinner."

Dominic went off, and Graine thought wistfully how beguiling it was to have some one care for one's simple comforts as his lordship did. How many men, she wondered would know or care that a guest might miss his dinner through the vicissitudes of travel?

She was roused from this sentimental reverie by his lordship's voice announcing quietly, "I am glad to have this opportunity of private speech with you, Miss Ashley. I have a matter of considerable importance to discuss."

Twelve

Graine waited expectantly, supposing that his lordship had some helpful suggestion to make with regard to Dominic's future. Instead he said slowly, "I had meant to seek an interview with you at my sister's house, but it occurs to me that there might be some difficulty in obtaining a measure of privacy, and I would not wish to embarrass you by displaying such particularity. So with your permission I will say what I have to say here and now, despite the fact that I once pledged you my word that you need not fear to be made the object of my attentions while you remained under my roof. At least you are no longer *residing* here, so I hold myself excused. And I do not ask for your answer immediately, only that you will hear me out patiently while we are alone. Then you may consider my plea at your leisure."

He fell silent a moment, wondering how best to put his case. Graine regarded him with startled eyes, the dawning of a great fear in her heart. Surely, oh, surely he was not going to make her an improper proposal. Yet that was what his words indicated.

She was a modest creature, Graine Ashley, and the vicissitudes of her working life had done nothing to foster any sense of her own importance. Even in dreams it had never entered her head that his lordship might fall so deep in love with her that he would offer her marriage. Acknowledging her own love for him, she also acknowledged its hopelessness, and the strenuous efforts that she had made of late to put the very thought of him out of her mind had only served to stiffen this attitude. There could be no honourable connection between them, so she must forget him. That he should think her the kind of girl who would consent to a clandestine liaison was a cruel blow. Her hands clenched involuntarily to contain the pain of it. She heard his words as though from a distance. This was not the man she had learned to love. That man would have known that such a suggestion could only hurt and insult her.

The quiet voice reached her in mid-phrase. "—that ridiculous masquerade, Miss Mouse. Even then you had won a place in my heart, though my promise obliged me to preserve an indifferent front. I find you completely adorable. So many little things. The way you wrinkle your nose when you are about to score a subtle hit; the droop of your lips in sympathy with some childish grief among your charges. I could go on for an age, but time presses. Perhaps some day I may be permitted to tell you all the ways in which I find you desirable, and essential to my happiness. Indeed I do not know how I shall go on without you if you decline my offer. Which is why I will not press you for an immediate answer. It is my hope that you are not entirely indifferent to me, and that when you search your heart you may even find it possible to return the feeling that I have for you. I cannot help thinking that the way in which you guarded my interests while I was in Copenhagen and the support and advice that you gave so generously after my return are indications that encourage me to hope."

He studied her face, his eyes eager, his manner diffident. There was no response. He sighed, and continued, "At the same time, it is your happiness that I desire above everything and I am only too well aware that a closer relationship between us is fraught with certain difficulties."

For a moment he thought of mentioning the disparity in age. But she probably knew of it already and why should he argue against his own cause? Instead he said temperately, "On the other hand I can offer several advantages. You would have a life of comfort and consideration. No more need to earn your bread in servitude. What would doubtless weigh more with *you*, you would be able to help Dominic to the kind of occupation that will suit him very much better than a clerk's stool, and possibly to forward the interests of your other brothers."

He put forward these arguments in all humility, trusting that his established position, the influence that he could wield, might in some sort off-set that fatal difference in age. Graine found it unbearable. That he should calmly list the advantages attached to the loss of her virtue! Did he really believe that either Dominic or his brothers would be content to profit by her descent into the muslin company? Or, indeed, that she herself would consider such a situation as anything other than velvet-cushioned servitude of the most degrading kind.

Once again the Earl studied the set little face with anxious eyes. He could detect no signs of thaw, but at least he knew better

than to offer further inducements that sa-
voured of bribery. He said soberly, "You need
not be thinking that you would be obliged to
lead an idle fashionable life with nothing
useful to do. I know you well enough to realise
that such an existence would not content you.
The wives and families of my people would
welcome your concern as they did during my
absence. There would be plenty to interest
and occupy you."

If she had not been personally involved,
Graine could have laughed in his face. In
some ways men were impossibly obtuse. Only
too well she could picture the reactions of respectable tenants' wives if the Earl's mistress
should presume to interest herself in their
affairs!

Seeing the first flicker of feeling on that
composed little face, his lordship wondered
if he dared venture to mention the possibility
of a family of their own. He decided against
it. It was too soon to speak of such intimate
matters. Besides, he thought it likely that for
the moment Graine had had her fill of children—other people's—and in any case he
could hear Dominic clattering down the staircase. The interlude of privacy was over.

Graine never knew how she got through
the rest of the visit. A rigid training in social
responsibilities stood her in good stead.
Somehow she managed to swallow a few

mouthfuls of the delicious meal that Mrs Palmer sent up to them, took a mechanical part in the conversation that accompanied it. The chaos of her thoughts could not be sifted here. She must have solitude. Meanwhile there were correct observances to be remembered, and Dominic's feelings, already strained by the exigencies of his own situation.

Valiantly she played her part, conversed, smiled, acknowledged, drew her brother into various discussions with only the haziest idea as to what they were about, and finally sank thankfully into Lady Elizabeth's carriage for the return to Town with his lordship's valediction ringing in her ears.

"I shall look forward to seeing you next Sunday."

The meeting loomed enormous and terrifying in her imagination. She would have to give him her answer. It must be refusal, of course, but how could she phrase it so as to hurt him as little as possible? However outrageous his suggestion, she still loved him, could not endure the thought of inflicting pain. Obviously he would be disappointed, but no more so, she told herself, than a child denied a coveted toy. Soon his fancy would light on some other female who might prove more amenable. He might even choose a bride. That, she discovered, was a thought that she did not care to contemplate for long.

She remembered those comfortable tea parties in the schoolroom at Valminster, and wished, foolishly, that she had been born a great heiress; one who might be thought a fitting bride for Valminster's lord. Because he loved her in his way. He had spoken quietly enough, had made no impassioned declarations, yet the sincerity of the appeal had tugged at her heart so that it would be difficult to deny him. For a moment she turned coward. Why should she not accept Mr Hughes's invitation to visit his mother on Sunday? But she dismissed the idea even as it entered her head. It would be unfair to use that pleasant young man as a shield, besides possibly arousing quite unfounded hopes in his heart. She even thought of asking if she might go and visit Bridie, but that idea, too, was dismissed. What was the good of evading the issue? Sooner or later it would have to be faced. The thing to do was to concentrate on the choice of courteous phrases in which to decline his lordship's offer.

The difficulty was that there were no such words. Even in a haphazard establishment like the Ashley's, the education of a young lady had included the learning by heart of the correct phrases in which to accept or reject a proposal of marriage. But very naturally, methods of dealing with the offer of a carte blanche had not been thought neces-

sary. It did not take Graine long to decide
that there *was* no tactful way of doing it.
What shocked her deeply was the discovery
that, despite the strict moral code in which
she had been reared, despite her own initial
revulsion, her refusal was less than whole-
hearted. There was never any doubt that she
would refuse, but some small rebellious part
of her inmost being clamoured to bestow upon
her love any comfort or happiness that was
within her gift. If she had been quite alone
in the world she might even have yielded to
his lordship's persuasions. But there were her
brothers and Bridie and even the small new
Jonathon. All of them would be slurred by
her disgrace, suffer from a scandal that would
rock Society, and all of them totally innocent
and helpless to avert it. She could not bring
herself to plunge them all into social disaster
for her own selfish gratification.

Once again she wondered desolately why
circumstance had not chosen to make her a
fitting bride for his lordship, and then realised suddenly that even that would not have
satisfied her. She wanted him to love her—
yes. But not because she was suitable. He
must love her as she loved him—helplessly,
desperately, despite her best endeavours and
regardless of suitability. She decided that it
was impossible to rehearse the shattering
scene that might develop on Sunday. She

need remember only two things. To be as calm and courteous as possible and to persist in saying no. The rest would depend upon his lordship. Meanwhile one had to go on living with some appearance of normality. She shook up her pillow, thumped it into a different shape, and settled herself for a night of restless slumber much haunted by dreams.

Once again work was her best solace. When she was with the children their demands obliged her to concentrate on them. For a little while she could push aside the thought of the difficult interview that lay ahead of her. When she was alone it was not so easy. She tried to plan for her future. It was manifestly impossible for her to remain in Lady Elizabeth's service once she had given Lord Valminster his congé. In comparison with the broken heart that was a minor sorrow, but it was still a sorrow, for she was sincerely attached to the children and to Beatrice, and warmly appreciative of Lady Elizabeth's kindness and consideration. Perhaps her heart was not broken after all, she thought wryly, for the vestige of a sense of humour still remained. Perhaps she was just in that mood of disenchantment with the world that had caused the mediaeval maiden to betake herself to a nunnery. In modern times one could scarcely do *that*, but a ladies' seminary would provide a very good substitute. No time there to repine for a lost dream of love. Her own old governess now ran a very select establishment in Bath. She would write to Miss Lavery forthwith and enquire if she had a vacancy for a junior governess.

Sunday came, inevitably. She went to church with the children, but for once she took little comfort from the peaceful rhythm of the service. They walked home through the Park, but she was nervous and distracted so that Adam and Bridget stared at her curiously when she returned absent-minded answers to their queries about the ducks on the pond. The children took luncheon with their parents, since for once there were no visitors. It was a pleasantly informal meal, but Graine had no appetite. Lady Elizabeth commented on this, asking kindly if she was over-tired or had the headache, and suggesting that she lie down on her bed for an hour. Graine thanked her but declined. Sooner or later she must face his lordship. It had better be sooner.

His lordship, for his part, had decided that it was time to be done with roundaboutation. Having duly greeted his sister and enquired after Sir John's progress, he abandoned manoeuvre and told his sister quite bluntly the purpose of his visit, requesting the favour of half an hour's private conversation with Miss Ashley. Her patent delight in his intention was pleasing, though he did not share her cheerful confidence in a happy outcome. He had not been unaware of Graine's lack of response to his overtures. To be sure he had said that he would not press for an immediate answer; that she should have time to consider well before committing herself. But if she had been deep in love with him she would not have availed herself of this opportunity. She would have flung herself into his eager arms there and then. The best he could hope for was that further consideration would have given weight to the advantages that he could offer, and that was cold comfort for a man in his state. By the time that Graine came to him in the Ladies' Parlour, he was quite as tense and nervous as she was, though he had himself well in hand and greeted her with his usual grave courtesy.

Presumably she responded adequately, though she could not afterwards have told any interested party what either of them had said. There was a brief pause while they regarded each other steadily and each took a deep breath. The ridiculous thought flashed across his lordship's mind that they were more like two duellists awaiting the drop of the handkerchief than a pair of lovers on the brink of a happy dénouement. His heart sank as he noted Graine's wary expression, but he would not draw back now. He put out a hand

and took her cold fingers in his, bowing low over them, though he did not kiss them as he would have liked to do. He would usurp no privileges until she granted him the right to them.

"Have you an answer for me, Miss Ashley," he said.

Graine's head went up proudly. "I have, sir," she answered steadily. "If it causes you chagrin I am sorry for it, but my answer is no."

He had been in part prepared for her refusal, but the manner of it took him aback. He had always been given to understand that young ladies invariably treated an offer of marriage as a compliment, even if the suitor was totally ineligible or simply not just to their liking. To receive a blunt 'no' from the usually gentle-mannered Graine, without any soothing remarks about the honour he had done her and her regret at being obliged to tell him that she felt they would not suit, was so unusual as to arouse his suspicions. Something was wrong. Perhaps she had heard some story about him that had displeased her. His lordship, at the age of seven and thirty, was no Galahad. In his salad days he had enjoyed various light affairs with damsels of even lighter virtue. But that was years ago. Surely a sensible girl like Graine Ashley would not hold that against him? For the rest, he hoped he was as decent a fellow as the next man, fair dealing to the best of his ability, generous when his heart was touched. Possibly someone had maligned him. Certainly the matter would bear investigation. That curt 'no' was like a slap in the face, but his lordship was not a man to give up at the first rebuff. He did not wish to distress the child, but there was a life-time's happiness at stake and he would venture to probe a little further.

He said slowly, "If I were a gentleman, Miss Ashley, I suppose I would accept my disappointment with stoicism and would trouble you no more. It seems, alas, that I am not. Have I displeased you in some way? Is there something in my habits or character that you find utterly unacceptable? For I would do my utmost to mend such matters."

Graine was cast into complete confusion. It had taken all her determination to pronounce that abrupt refusal to his face, when all she had wanted to do was to melt into his arms and promise that she would be all that he desired, so that she brought him happiness.

"No, indeed. There is nothing. Your lordship's character is quite admirable," she stumbled out.

"But you do not find yourself able to sustain the thought of living with me," he returned grimly. "Very well, ma'am, I accept my defeat. Now let us consider how I may take my leave with the least embarrassment to you. The devil is in it that I must stay overnight. Sir John and I have business affairs that will keep me in Town until tomorrow. It is obvious that my continued presence must be uncomfortable for you. In time, no doubt, we shall become accustomed, but for tonight—" he broke off and appeared to be wrapped in thought.

"I could keep my room," she said desperately. "Lady Elizabeth enquired at luncheon if I had the headache. No one would think it strange if I did not come down to dinner. So we could avoid any awkwardness. As for the future, I shall resign my post here. I have already written about another situation."

His lordship felt like a murderer. Where he had hoped to give her every care and luxury, he had cast her adrift. He knew that she had been happy with the Brownings. Now she must leave her comfortable situation, the blame to be laid at his door. He would find her a comparable post, he determined, even though she had refused to marry him, even if he had to fabricate one. A post where she could be as happy as she had been with the Brownings.

He said temperately, "That would seem a reasonable solution. And in the morning you will be busy with the children until after I have taken my departure."

But he did not immediately take his leave, standing looking down at her in contemplative fashion as though there was a good deal more that he would have liked to say. In actual fact he was conning the ranks of his acquaintance in search of a family who might have need of a governess, but his thoughtful air made her nervous, and nervousness drove her to revert to the very topic that she had meant at all costs to avoid.

"There could be no happiness in such a union as you suggested, milord," she said timidly. "The disparity between us could never be bridged. I could not have been the same person whom you singled out for your preference. Perhaps I seemed to you a little unusual, which caught your attention, but I am sure you will not long regret your disappointment when you consider the number of disagreeable problems in which you must have been involved."

He supposed her to be referring to Dominic's difficulties, to which he had already found an excellent solution. But since he also thought that the reference to disparity could only apply to the difference in age, he was not prepared to argue further. It was as he had thought, and knowing her situation he could only respect a decision that held no trace of self-interest, however much it hurt him personally.

"You cannot, of course, expect me to agree with you," he said with that delightful smile. "Indeed, I still nourish some faint hope that you will change your mind. But once again I find myself obliged to give you my word that I will not pester you with my solicitations. Only I beg that if you *do* change your mind you will not permit modesty or that sensitive pride of yours to prevent you from informing me. Surely that is a fair bargain? For despite your attempts to assure me that I shall soon forget you, I promise you that I shall not change mine. Moreover I hope that you will still regard me as a friend to whom you may bring any problems that trouble you. In the matter of Dominic's future, for instance," he began, and broke off short.

His kindness was the one thing needed to shatter her composure. The tears were rolling down her cheeks, though she made no attempt to turn her head away as she said huskily, "I am sorry, milord. Pray hold me excused," and turned and fled.

Thirteen

It was hours before she slept. She sent her supper tray away almost untouched, which brought Lady Elizabeth to see if she was seriously unwell. Her ladyship was kind but distant. Her brother had naturally been obliged to tell her that his suit had not prospered, and she had considerable difficulty in mastering her indignation to the point of speaking politely to the girl who had actually presumed to reject the most eligible bachelor in Town. Ross! Who had every card in the matrimonial stakes stacked in his favour. Rank—wealth—character. He would make the very nicest kind of husband thought his sister, with a good deal of justification. And

Graine Ashley had refused him. The girl's
wan little face and tear-swollen eyes did
something to soften her employer's heart, but
she could not bring herself to the point of
forgiveness. There could be no understanding
Miss Ashley's behaviour. But her brother had
straitly forbidden her to refer to the matter
so she confined her remarks to a suggestion
that the physician should be summoned if the
sufferer thought she might be sickening for
the influenza, of which there was a good deal
about, and, when this proposal was firmly
negatived, Graine declaring that she ailed no
more than a severe headache which would be
mended by a night's sleep, to the offer of a
few drops of laudanum. She insisted that Beatrice bring the bottle from her room but
agreed that it would be better if Miss Ashley
could sleep naturally. Graine, a healthy creature who never ailed anything, was a little
frightened of powerful drugs since she had
never had cause to use them. She tried every
time-honoured method of wooing the sleep
that could bring her blessed forgetfulness for
a time. But neither counting sheep nor the
recitation of French verbs sufficed to drive
his lordship's image from her mind. And she
saw him, of course, as he had looked when
they parted, his face grave but full of kindly
concern as he began to speak of Dominic's
future, and could have wept anew. How could

she ever hope to understand him? How could
the same man make improper proposals to
the sister and yet, even though they were
rejected, concern himself with the affairs of
a youngster who had no shadow of a claim on
him?

Between this recurring vision and thoughts
of a future in which his lordship had no part
to play, it was little wonder that sheep and
recitation stood small chance of success. Towards midnight she re-made her tumbled
bed, measured out a few drops of the opiate
which she sipped with mingled doubt and
distaste, and composed herself once more for
slumber. This time she *did* sleep, heavily and
uneasily, but she slept.

She also dreamed; so vividly that she could
recall a good deal of the dream when she
woke. In the dream she was walking in a
forest. It was very dark and the trees were
gnarled and ancient. No birds sang. The still-
ness was so oppressive that she grew frightened. The twisted branches seemed to spread
cruel fingers to clutch at her and hinder her
passage. They caught in her hair and clothing. She struggled to free herself, only to be
held helplessly so that fear turned to panic.
A stand of trees ahead of her burst suddenly
into flames and she fought desperately to escape from the prisoning branches that held
her at their mercy; fought so desperately that

she woke, to find herself once again entangled in the bedclothes.

The dream still possessed her imagination. She could even smell the smoke from the burning trees, so strongly that it was choking. That's the last time that I take laudanum, she vowed in exasperation, and then realised that the smoke was no dream. Something was burning. The smoke was real and was growing thicker every moment.

She struggled out of bed, still hazy with the remnants of drugged slumber, and began to pull on her clothes, hurriedly, any how. This must be investigated. It might be only a chimney fire, but it was an odd time for such a mishap she thought, her brain clearing with every active movement that she made. There could be danger. It was even possible that the house was on fire. That last thought accelerated her movements. The children! No one else seemed to have been alarmed by the smell of smoke, for all was quiet. She dispensed with the formality of stockings and gown and pulled on her slippers and a loose wrapper that needed no hooking up.

As she opened her bedroom door she could see that the smoke was thicker in the corridor. She turned back and tugged at the bell pull, jerkily, fiercely. It would sound some sort of alarm she hoped, picked up her candle and set off for the children's rooms. It might have been more sensible to rouse Sir John and Lady Elizabeth, but in her still slightly dazed state her only thought was for the children who were her responsibility.

The schoolroom floor was only slightly tainted with the smell of smoke. It was possible to breathe freely, but Bridget and Adam were sleeping rather more soundly than usual and objected to being roused and bidden to dress at such an unseasonable hour. She left them drowsily obeying her commands and went to rouse Beatrice whose room was at the other end of the corridor. Here the smoke was much thicker, so much so that she was seriously alarmed. Beatrice was deeply asleep. She set this bell, too, pealing violently and shook the girl into wakefulness, huddled her into her clothes and bade her go down to waken her parents, while she herself went back to shepherd the younger children to safety.

The house awoke to sudden, unnatural life. The family gathered in the hall, the children divided between excitement and awe, Sir John giving orders with crisp authority. A man was sent running to summon the parish fire brigade, others to ensure that all the servants were awake and aware of the danger. Lady Elizabeth suggested that it might be wise to remove small valuables to a place of safety, but Sir John said that there was little danger of a serious fire. The outbreak was at present confined to his study, and thanks to the early warning given by Miss Ashley he thought that their own servants and the firemen would have no difficulty in bringing it under control. His wife stared at him—and shrieked.

"Ross! I put him in the room over your study, because his usual room is rather cold at this time of year. Oh! If anything has happened to him, I shall never forgive myself."

Sir John, who had forgotten all about his brother-in-law, made for the main staircase at his best speed. Graine Ashley was quicker. At the news that Lord Valminster was in the room immediately above the fire, she forgot everything except his danger. He must have been stupified by the smoke, might even now be suffocating. She could picture the flames already licking at the floor of his room. Young Benedict had once formed the opinion that Miss Ashley could move swiftly enough if occasion demanded. She had never moved faster. Regardless of her rather exiguous attire she brushed past Sir John—still limping a little from his injury—without ceremony, her wrapper streaming behind her, and raced up the stairs to his lordship's room to fling open the door and learn the worst without delay.

Lord Valminster had gone late to his bed, having spent the evening with Sir John in the study, thankful to seek distraction from his personal problems in discussing various matters of mutual interest, in blowing a cloud (and thereby, between them, causing all the present alarm and excitement) and in sampling his host's excellent brandy a good deal more freely than was his normal custom. Probably it was the depth of his potations that had caused him to sleep soundly through the initial alarm. Certainly he did not wake until the unusual noises produced by the arrival of the fire brigade penetrated his peaceful slumber. He was still not alarmed. Some freak current of air had prevented the smoke from invading his room to an extent that made it immediately noticeable. He just wanted to know who had arrived at this hour of the morning with such jingling of harness and ringing of bells.

He lit his candle and climbed out of bed in leisurely fashion, yawned, stretched and took off his nightcap. He was in the act of pulling on an exotic looking dressing gown when his bedroom door was flung open with some violence and the unpredictable Miss Ashley appeared on the threshold.

For a moment he stared, unable to believe his eyes, wondering if he was still asleep and dreaming. Miss Ashley did not at first perceive him because he was standing in the far corner of the room behind the circle of light cast by the candle. She ran across to the bed, flinging back the curtain to discover that there was no occupant, and lifted her head in anxious search.

His lordship was no slow-top. Whatever had brought her here in this unconventional fashion, he must learn its cause at once. He had already started towards her when she saw him. In a passion of relief that he was alive and safe when she had feared him dead or at least in grave danger, she flung herself into his arms. They were not unreceptive. His kiss was pressed on her mouth almost before she was aware. Her feeble defences crumbled. She returned the kiss and clung as though he was her sole dependence, while he folded her protectively close. A pretty sight to meet the eyes of Sir John, entering the room only a few seconds behind Miss Ashley, and both participants barely decently dressed. Fortunately he was a gentleman of wide tolerance in certain aspects, and not devoid of humour. His wife having apprised him of how matters stood between her brother and Miss Ashley, he began to detect the finger of providence in the fire that had wrecked his study. No serious damage had been done, no one was hurt, and at least, he decided, hiding a grin, he would have a pretty tale to tell his wife

if she began to upbraid him for the careless-
ness with the smouldering end of his cheroot
which had probably caused the conflagration.
In his opinion—and he was something of a
judge—the pair so raptly locked in each
other's arms that they had not even noticed
his arrival, were in a fair way to settling their
difficulties, if they had not already done so.
It was really quite a pity to interrupt them,
but he had left his wife in a state of considerable anxiety about her brother's safety,
which he must relieve as soon as possible.
Nor did he think that Elizabeth, something
of a high stickler where morals were concerned, would approve of this bedroom tête-
à-tête.

With the tact to be expected of an experienced diplomat he said pleasantly, "I think
this floor is growing unpleasantly warm,
Ross. And since the door was opened the
smoke is beginning to creep up through the
floor boards. Oh! Nothing serious or alarm-
ing, you understand. Just a small fire in the
study. One of us must have been careless, I
fear. The firemen are dealing very compe-
tently, but I think we would be more comfortable downstairs. It would really be very
awkward if this floor collapsed and precipi-
tated the three of us into the embers below."

He politely held open the door to allow Miss
Ashley to precede him from the room, and

Lord Valminster released her with a final reassuring hug. There was nothing he could usefully say to her in the presence of a third party, but he was no longer in any doubt as to the state of her feelings and meant to have a sensible explanation from her before he left Town. He was very happy, for he knew now that whatever misguided scruples had persuaded her to refuse him, she loved him as much—or almost as much—as he loved her. He had only to coax her to explain her reasons and then they could arrange matters openly. He began to wonder how soon they could be married, but the welcome from the family who were looking anxiously for his appearance and came crowding round him with little ejaculations of relief and greeting served to distract his thoughts. Only his sister was a little surprised by his obvious high spirits. Perhaps they might be attributed to his escape from a potentially dangerous situation, but she rather thought not. She remembered how Graine had fled up the stairs at the thought of that danger and studied that damsel searchingly, but Graine's face gave nothing away. She was engaged in answering Adam's questions about the progress and direction of the fire, explaining how it needed air to fan it into real ferocity and using the homely bellows as an illustration of this truth. Feeling her employer's eye upon her she asked if she should now settle the children down for what was left of the night. Hot milk and biscuits, she suggested, might persuade them to abandon the scene of action. In any case there was not much more to be seen. The firemen were packing up their equipment. Their leader, who was a senior clerk with the fire insurance company, was solemnly warning Sir John of the dangers of smoking indoors, an attitude fully endorsed by Lady Elizabeth, but relaxed into a more benevolent attitude when it was suggested that he and his men might appreciate some refreshment after their labours. Fire fighting, he admitted, was thirsty work. A drop of ale would not come amiss.

He and his men departed kitchenward, and since Lady Elizabeth would not permit the children to go outside to see the horses that pulled the fire engine, Graine was able quite easily to persuade them back to bed.

Graine's own feelings were mixed. Paramount was gratitude that no one had suffered injury. But no amount of recalling the exact circumstances could blind her to the fact that her demonstration of relief at his lordship's survival had been excessive. She had betrayed herself completely and she knew it. After such encouragement he might well renew his importunities and the whole sorry business would be to do again. She dwelt for a moment on the memory of that one illicit kiss, shook her head vigorously as though by so doing she could banish it, and climbed into bed. Tomorrow seemed likely to be a difficult day. She had better snatch what sleep she could if she was to bring her usual calm good sense to bear on the problems that she saw looming ahead.

Fourteen

As a result of their disturbed night, every one was slightly out of frame next morning. Graine was tense and anxious. She would not breathe easily until she knew that his lordship had taken his departure. Beatrice was heavy-eyed and inclined to be pettish, vowing that she felt much too tired to practise that dull sonata and would certainly fall asleep if she was required to study her Italian lesson. Adam and Bridget took their tone from her and were fractious and troublesome. Graine could only be thankful when Lady Elizabeth came into the schoolroom half way through the morning and decreed a holiday for the rest of the day.

Her manner this morning was warmly friendly, Sir John having favoured her with a slightly expurgated account of the scene that he had witnessed in his brother-in-law's bedroom. After puzzling over it for some time she had come to the pleasing conclusion that Graine had refused his lordship's proposal out of modesty. The girl had not thought herself good enough for him, had probably believed that his family and friends would unite in disapproval of so unequal a match, and though obviously she loved him to desperation she had refused him rather than bring such trouble about his head. It was a ridiculously romantic attitude but to Lady Elizabeth it was understandable. Her plan now was to encourage Graine to pluck up heart by displaying the very real liking that she, Ross's closest relation, had for her. So she scolded the children, though in a teasing sort of way, for being so troublesome to Miss Ashley, who had saved them all from being burned in their beds by her timely warning of danger, and vowed that they did not deserve the treat that she had planned for them.

"I mean to drive out to Kew this afternoon to visit your Grandmama," she told them. "The news of last night's fire is bound to reach her, as news always does reach the persons whom one would particularly wish to remain in ignorance, and she will be anxious for all of us. I plan to be beforehand and tell her about it myself. You shall all come with me, and that will give poor Miss Ashley an afternoon of peace. Would you not like to visit your sister, my dear? She, too, may like to be reassured as to your safety."

Graine accepted with sincere gratitude. Such an excursion was just what she needed. It would take her out of the house until after his lordship had left it. She knew already that he was occupied with Sir John this morning. He had told her so himself. With reasonable good fortune it might be weeks before he came up to Town again. By then she could be safely hidden away in a seminary in Bath, if Miss Lavery's answer to her application was favourable. It was not exactly an exciting prospect, but anything was better than being obliged to meet his lordship again before the memory of last night's shameful encounter had been allowed to fade. When Lady Elizabeth suggested that she should lie down on her bed and rest until luncheon because she looked pale and tired after her disturbed night and very understandably, too, she could have hugged her. When her benefactress further suggested that she might like to lunch quietly in her own room, away from the chatter of the children, she was able to relax completely. One might almost have thought that Lady Elizabeth knew how she was situated and sympathised with her difficulties. She bestowed such a speaking look of gratitude upon her employer that Lady Elizabeth, whose benevolence was not quite so disinterested as it appeared, felt positively guilty. She promptly dismissed this ridiculous scruple. After all, was she not acting in Graine's own best interests? Instead of nourishing doubts about her activities she should be pluming herself on the success of her enterprise. These affairs only needed a little thought and diplomacy, she reflected.

Her mind more or less at peace, Graine fell asleep almost at once and awoke much refreshed to enjoy the luncheon that Susie brought her and to drink the glass of wine that had been sent up with it. She felt a new person, able to face the world again, able even to take pleasure in as beautiful a day as March ever borrowed from May. Lady Elizabeth and the children would have a delightful drive down to Kew, she thought, and was glad for them. She herself would enjoy the walk to Bridie's.

In this comparatively carefree mood she came down the main staircase a little after two, dressed for the visit in one of her sober brown day dresses but paying tribute to the beauty of the day by wearing a rather charming bonnet in burnt straw, tied beneath her chin with a brown satin ribbon. She glanced about her a little apprehensively but no one was about. Boulding, Sir John's butler, emerged from the slip of a room where he usually lurked when he was not busy in his pantry and bade her good afternoon. He proceeded to discourse on such varying topics as last night's fire, the dangers of smoking indoors, the work that would have to be done to put the study to rights and the beauty of the weather. She was a little surprised. Though always polite and respectful, Boulding was not normally garrulous. He was a man of middle age, very professional, with none of the relaxed friendliness of the old family servant. She could only think that the events of the previous night had put him all on end, or even that he was grateful for her own small efforts. She answered and commiserated and agreed as seemed suitable, and assured him pleasantly that she was in no great haste when he eventually apologised for delaying her and moved forward majestically to open the door.

The shock of seeing Lord Valminster's curricle drawn up outside, the curricle that she had pictured as on its homeward way an hour ago, seemed to deprive her of her senses. Before she well knew what she was about, Boulding had handed her up into the seat beside the driver, and his lordship, having tucked a rug over her knees, was giving his horses the office.

"I thought you would not object to an open carriage on so mild a day," he said pleasantly while still she strove for breath. "So long as we take it gently I think you will be warm enough, and at least the fresh air will drive last night's smoke out of your lungs."

This matter-of-fact approach did something to reassure her until she realised that his lordship had dismissed his groom, so that they were quite alone with no one to hear what passed between them, and that he was certainly not following the usual route to her sister's house. She had walked it on several occasions and knew it well. But when she broke silence to question if he had mistaken the way, his reply was forthright in the extreme.

"No, Miss Ashley, I have not. Not today, at least, though I seem to have done so in the past. You and I have a good deal to say to one another on a matter of vital importance. Our—er—encounter in the small hours convinced me that I have totally misread the situation between us. I have come to believe that you love me as much as I love you. After your behaviour last night you cannot well deny it. Very well, then. Either someone has made mischief between us, which seems unlikely, or there is some misunderstanding.

We are not going to visit your excellent sister, Miss Ashley. She is not expecting you so she will not be disappointed, and a message has been dispatched to her assuring her of your safety after last night's drama. You climbed into my curricle of your own free will, under the eyes of several highly interested witnesses, but it is only fair to inform you that you have been abducted ma'am, and that I intend to hold you prisoner here by the very simple principle of driving on and on until we have reached a clear understanding. I am not driving my own horses, you will notice. These are hirelings—a sturdy, placid pair who will demand little of my attention, so that I can devote most of it to you. Such forethought, you will agree, speaks well for my sagacity, a useful quality in a prospective husband. You, I profoundly trust, will display a matching measure of compassion, and will consent to my offer of marriage before the wretched animals are driven to foundering point."

Graine gasped and nearly choked. Marriage! The idea had never entered her head. Could he have meant marriage all the time? Then why had he not said so? She was in no mood to appreciate the subtle compliment implied by his obvious belief that no man would have offered her less. Instinct might bid her fall into his arms—difficult in any case when he was driving, even *these* biddable animals—but oddly enough indignation took precedence. If only he had made his intentions clear, all this agonising could have been spared.

The indignation was possibly irrational, but it was very real. It caused her to say crisply, "That is blackmail, sir. And I should have no hesitation in breaking a promise extracted by such discreditable methods."

He glanced down at her briefly, but the burnt straw bonnet hid most of her face. All he could see, since her gaze was bent on the clasped hands lying in her lap, was the curve of one cheek and a mouth set in a mutinous line. It made him decide to tread warily.

"Be patient with me a little. I hope to win your forgiveness for my rather high-handed action in carrying you off like this. Simply, I was desperate, and desperate men use the first means to hand."

She neither spoke nor raised her head. A little encouraged, he went on. "When you declined to marry me it was a bitter blow. I did not expect you to love me as deeply and helplessly as I love you. I know that I am too old to figure as a young woman's beau ideal of romance. But I thought that we had learned to like and trust each other to the point where love might gradually follow. When you told me that there could be no hope of happiness in such a union, that the disparity between us could never be bridged, I accepted your decision with the deepest regret and assured you that if ever you changed your mind you would find me waiting. The events which took place last night gave me cause to think that perhaps you *had* changed your mind. You could not expect me to go meekly back to Valminster without trying my fortune once more."

The demure little creature seated beside him pressed one hand to her breast as though to still a wildly beating heart. Warm waves of delight and happiness were coursing through her whole body. He loved her. He wanted to marry her. All the dreams that she had never dared to indulge were going to come true. But although all she wanted was to yield to this flood of delightful emotions, there was one awkward obstacle. How was she to explain her own capricious behaviour? His lordship had spoken politely of 'changing her mind'. But she did not want him to think her a volatile, changeable creature who did not know what she wanted of life. She knew very well—had known for months—but had never expected to have it offered to her. How was she to explain the circumstances? It was not easy to tell a man that you had believed him to be offering you a carte blanche, which naturally you had been obliged to refuse. Did you tell him that it had been a sore temptation? That only consideration for the rest of your family had given you the strength to resist? Or did you tell him nothing at all, leaving him to suppose that you *had* simply changed your mind?

That was a coward's way out, and she revolted from it immediately. To tell anything less than the truth was to destroy the whole fabric on which their relationship was based. So, very well. The truth it must be. And how did one phrase it?

She made one false start. "When we discussed this matter in the library at Valminster I understood that—that your lordship was offering me"—Her tongue refused to form the words. She tried again. "I did not know that you had matrimony in mind," she said baldly.

The lean brown fingers that held the reins tightened involuntarily. The horses obediently dropped to a walk. His lordship said nothing, but if ever a silence was eloquent, his was, tense with unspoken fury. And presently he checked the horses, and regardless of the narrowness of the way began to back and turn them, his face so thunderous that Graine felt an odd little quiver of alarm.

"What are you going to do?" she demanded breathlessly.

"I am taking you home," he said curtly.

"Somewhere where I can get my hands on you. A good shaking is the least you deserve, my girl, daring to talk such stuff. If I had known what maggot was in your head I would never have brought you out. At worst I thought some idle mischief-maker had interfered to set you against me. I certainly never dreamed that the mischief was in your own mind. What had I ever done that you should malign me so? No thought of matrimony, indeed—and I thinking of nothing else since first I recognised your quality."

He relapsed into fuming silence. Graine took heart. He certainly sounded very cross, but she did not think that he was meditating casting her off because of her folly, and so long as *that* was all right, nothing else mattered. And she thought that he was probably finding some relief for his fury in the pace at which he was driving. Several people had turned to stare after them. If she wished to speak in her own defence she had best make haste, for at this rate they would be home in ten minutes.

She said tartly, "When you were so good as to inform me that you found me desirable and essential to your happiness—those were the exact words that you used, milord—you also spoke of the advantages that you could offer to a penniless governess, and of the difficulties consequent upon a closer relationship between us. Not once did you mention marriage, nor even say that you loved me. What else did you expect me to think?"

His lordship, drawing breath to annihilate this ridiculous argument, was pulled up short. He had, of course, expected her to think that he was offering marriage, and could scarcely believe that the word itself had never passed his lips. But if Graine said that it had not, he supposed, reluctantly, that there were some grounds for her misunderstanding. Then he remembered that she had passed a whole week under that same misapprehension without doing anything to clear the matter up, and fury rose again within him. He did not ask himself what a modest, gently bred girl *could* have done in such circumstances but nursed his wrath in silence until they drove into the mews, tossed the reins to a startled groom who eyed the sweating horses in shocked disbelief, and helped his passenger to alight, drawing her arm through his with a resolution that brooked no argument and conducting her into the house with all the air of a triumphant jailer who has just discovered his most prized prisoner in an attempt at escape.

He closed the drawing room door behind them with a firmness that convinced Boulding that an offer of refreshment at this juncture would be ill-timed, and took both her hands in his, spreading them wide so that she stood breast to breast with him. She yielded submissively, which seemed to have a soothing effect, though his face still wore a harsh expression that was unfamiliar to her. Just so, she thought, he might have looked at some enemy or opponent. It was a strange expression for the face of love.

He said slowly, as though he was biting out each word, "Miss Ashley, will you do me the honour of accepting my hand in marriage?"

Graine looked up into the beloved face. The harsh lines were softening, though he still looked deeply serious. If she had felt a momentary impulse to tease him by adopting a formality to match his own, it was banished by that expression.

"I never hoped to know such happiness, milord," she said simply. "If you truly feel that marriage with me is 'essential to *your* happiness'"—there was a little smile for the quotation—"then I consent willingly and proudly."

She was swept into his arms and soundly kissed almost before the words were out of her mouth, after which his lordship picked her up bodily, installed himself in one of his sister's comfortable chairs and drew her down to sit on his lap, "As though I were a little girl," she protested.

"Not much bigger—and certainly no more sensible," he told her severely.

"*Much* more sensible," she contradicted briskly. "Have I not just demonstrated my good sense by accepting your very obliging offer? To cast doubt upon it in the very moment when I have agreed to marry you must surely indicate that I am accepting something of little worth. Fortunately there can be two opinions about that, and I hold by my own, sensible or not."

Her happiness was bubbling over. She could not refrain from teasing him a little, putting on her prim 'governess' face as she said, "And you, my dear sir, must learn to set a higher value on yourself. The world, you know, is all too ready to accept us at our own valuation. It does not *do* to be too modest."

That made him chuckle. He gave her a loving little shake and declared that at least love and the imminent prospect of marriage had not made her maudlin.

"The astringent touch is something that I particularly enjoy in your remarks," he told her fondly, and kissed her again.

Fifteen

"*But we can't possibly* get married as soon as that!" exclaimed Graine in startled accents.

"Indeed we can," returned the Earl calmly. "Far too much time has been wasted already. If we delay any longer I shall have you changing your mind, and deciding that you are not going to throw yourself away on one so far sunk in senility."

Graine giggled. It would have been difficult to imagine any one less senile looking than his lordship, immaculate even in riding dress, his tall, spare figure obviously charged with springing vitality as he strode up and down his sister's breakfast parlour haranguing the ladies who were still lingering over their coffee. As a matter of fact they, too, had been discussing wedding plans, but Graine did not propose to tell him that.

"We must give your sister time to find someone to fill my place," she pointed out. "That is the least I can do after all the kindness she has shown me."

"No one could fill your place," pronounced Lady Elizabeth. "I shall, in any case, have to make do with some inferior substitute. It seems to me that the greatest service you can render me is to marry this impatient wretch as soon as may be. At least it will prevent him from wearing out my carpet by this endless pacing."

Her hearers chuckled, but Graine said, "Three weeks is much too soon. If you only knew how sick I am of wearing dingy greys and browns. At least I would like to appear becomingly dressed on my wedding day. Give me time to choose a pretty dress."

"Three weeks is time and enough," returned the Earl firmly. "Nor do you need all the trappings of fashion to appear at your best. I have not forgotten how you looked at Christmas in a dress of some dark red stuff, and though it may put my sister to the blush I will take leave to tell you that I have never seen you look lovelier than you did with no more than a dressing gown pulled over your petticoat."

As Graine blushed and Lady Elizabeth exclaimed, he added reflectively, "That was the moment when I knew that you *did* love me after all. I daresay you would have looked beautiful in sackcloth. But we digress. Three weeks. Time to have the banns called—no need even for a special licence, so you cannot complain of undue haste—and then a quiet wedding at Valminster. Unless you prefer to be married from your sister's house."

The date of the wedding having apparently been settled by this determined gentleman, both ladies agreed that Valminster would afford more scope for the necessary entertainment. Lady Elizabeth began to enumerate all the people who simply *must* be invited, and announced that she would play hostess for her brother, and although the Earl protested that he had stipulated for a quiet wedding, this time he was over-ruled.

"Do you want the family to think that you are ashamed of your bride?" demanded his sister, which put an end to further argument.

"And Beatrice shall be your bride's maiden," Lady Elizabeth went on happily, "which will give her a great deal of pleasure and do her a great deal of good."

His lordship demanding enlightenment on this head was told that it was just the kind of formal appearance that was invaluable for a budding débutante. "She will be in the public eye without being the central figure, and she will have no time to be nervous about her own appearance," said Lady Elizabeth simply. "Who will you have for your groomsman?"

"Dominic," returned his lordship promptly. "He is a little young for such a responsible position, but no younger than Bea, and he did more than any one to bring us about when it began to look as though all was at an end."

His sister cried out at that. "And who took the children down to Kew and arranged everything so that you could have Rainey all to yourself yesterday afternoon?" she demanded indignantly, forgetting that Graine was unawared of this innocent little plot. But Graine was too happy to care and only laughed when she learned that half the household had been involved, from Susie, who had smuggled out to the curricle a warm pelisse done up in a neat parcel in case the weather should change, to Boulding, whose task was to delay Miss Ashley in the hall until there was time for the curricle to come round from the mews. Even the Earl grinned at the recital of all the topics that his sister had suggested to the taciturn Boulding as suitable subjects for conversation with a young lady supposedly setting out to visit her sister.

But Graine's thoughts were turning to

more serious subjects. The mention of Dominic reminded her that she had not seen her brother since they had visited Valminster together.

"Dominic will be happy for us," she said thoughtfully. "And though I expect we shall spend most of our time at Valminster, we shall be able to see a good deal of him when we are in Town. That is, if he decides to accept Mr Sutcliffe's offer."

"You will see a good deal more of him while we are at Valminster," retorted her betrothed. "That is, if he decides to accept *my* offer rather than Mr Sutcliffe's."

Both ladies turned to him eagerly. He said slowly, "From a financial point of view his prospects would not compare with those that Mr Sutcliffe can offer. But if he has no real aptitude for business, would those prospects ever materialise? If he comes to me he would be living the kind of life that he likes and making a decent livelihood as well. A couple of years working under Oliver to teach him the ropes and then a spell with Franklin on the Leicestershire estates. Franklin is getting on towards retiring and it's time we were training up someone to succeed him. Mind you, I make no promises about that—shan't even mention it to the boy—but I think he's got the right stuff in him. He likes the country way of life and gets on well with country

people. And for a boy of seventeen he's got a
strong sense of responsibility. What do you
think?"

"He'll jump at it," said Graine quietly, but
her eyes glowed with gratitude. "It is just the
kind of thing that he will like above everything. He'll work hard, too. Not only because
he likes the work but because he'll be so determined to prove that he is really equal to
it and not just hanging on your sleeve."

The Earl grinned. "That I can well believe.
I've met the same sort of pride in his sister,
who would never permit me to do anything
to smooth her path but always preferred to
manage for herself."

Graine burst into indignant protest. Lady
Elizabeth smiled indulgently and, on the pre-
text that, with a wedding to arrange so soon
she had a great deal to do, tactfully whisked
herself out of the room.

The Earl was not one to waste opportunity.
The door had scarcely closed behind her before he had gathered Graine into his hold.
She looked up at him trustfully. There was
a slight delay while he kissed her, as he said,
properly, as opposed to the chaste salute that
he had dropped upon her cheek when he came
in from his ride. Graine chuckled and announced that she did not think much of his
notions of propriety. But since she then added
thoughtfully that she very much enjoyed his

kisses, proper or not, he was not noticeably dashed down.

Presently he returned to some semblance of order. "It is hard to have to leave you, my darling. But as Elizabeth so truly said, with a wedding to be arranged so soon, there is a great deal to be done, and as you know, I should really have gone back to Valminster yesterday. Moreover I want to see Dominic before I go back to put my proposition to him. Then he can think it over at his leisure."

She laughed. "Small need of that! What a pity it is that gentlemen are so undemonstrative. I daresay he will want to hug you, but his notions of proper behaviour will not permit him to do so. I am very glad that I am a female."

His lordship, indicating that he concurred with this opinion, provided some evidence that all gentlemen are not always undemonstrative.

She snuggled confidingly in his hold. It was in a rather shaken voice that he said, "Almost you persuade me that I am not so ancient after all. Tell me, little love. I promise that I will not bother you with further heart searchings, but just this once. Do you truly feel that I am not too old for you? You are so young, so bewitching. You could have any one."

There could be only one answer to that.

Graine put up her hands to frame his face and tugged gently so that he stooped to her. She kissed him full on the mouth, the first time that she had done so uninvited, and into the kiss she put all the love and the longing that she had suppressed for so many weary weeks. As his arms closed about her, his lordship knew, once and for all, that he was not a day too old. He was exactly right.

THRILLS * CHILLS * MYSTERY
from FAWCETT BOOKS

NEW FROM FAWCETT CREST

☐ KANE & ABEL   24376 $3.75
   by Jeffrey Archer

☐ THE FEAST OF ALL SAINTS   24378 $2.95
   by Anne Rice

☐ LAST ACT   24379 $2.50
   by Jane Aiken Hodge

☐ KATHERINE   24381 $2.50
   by Antonia Van-Loon

☐ INSPIRING MESSAGES FOR DAILY LIVING   24383 $2.50
   by Norman Vincent Peale

☐ RESISTING ARREST   24386 $2.50
   by Steven Phillips

☐ CASEBOOK OF THE BLACK WIDOWERS   24384 $2.25
   by Isaac Asimov

☐ THE LAST IMMORTAL   24385 $2.25
   by J. O. Jeppson

Buy them at your local bookstore or use this handy coupon for ordering.

COLUMBIA BOOK SERVICE (a CBS Publications Co.)
32275 Mally Road, P.O. Box FB, Madison Heights, MI 48071

Please send me the books I have checked above. Orders for less than 5 books must include 75¢ for the first book and 25¢ for each additional book to cover postage and handling. Orders for 5 books or more postage is FREE. Send check or money order only.

Cost $_____   Name _____

Sales tax*_____   Address _____

Postage_____   City _____

Total $_____   State _____ Zip _____

* The government requires us to collect sales tax in all states except AK, DE, MT, NH and OR.

This offer expires 1 December 81   8138

GREAT ADVENTURES IN READING

Let COVENTRY Give You
A Little Old-Fashioned Romance

☐ LADY BRANDY   50165 $1.75
   by Claudette Williams

☐ THE SWANS OF BRHYADR   50166 $1.75
   by Vivienne Couldrey

☐ HONORA CLARE   50167 $1.75
   by Sheila Bishop

☐ TWIST OF CHANCE   50169 $1.75
   by Elisabeth Carey

☐ THE RELUCTANT RIVALS   50170 $1.75
   by Georgina Grey

☐ THE MERCHANT'S
   DAUGHTER   50172 $1.75
   by Rachelle Edwards

Buy them at your local bookstore or use this handy coupon for ordering.

COLUMBIA BOOK SERVICE (a CBS Publications Co.)
32275 Mally Road, P.O. Box FB, Madison Heights, MI 48071

Please send me the books I have checked above. Orders for less than 5 books must include 75¢ for the first book and 25¢ for each additional book to cover postage and handling. Orders for 5 books or more postage is FREE. Send check or money order only.

Cost $_____   Name _____

Sales tax*_____   Address _____

Postage_____   City _____

Total $_____   State _____ Zip _____

*The government requires us to collect sales tax in all states except AK, DE, MT, NH and OR.

This offer expires 1 December 81   8136